THE BEST OF YOU

THE OCEANIC DREAMS SERIES BOOK EIGHT

SOPHIE-LEIGH ROBBINS

The Best of You

©2019 by Sophie-Leigh Robbins

All Rights Reserved

Cover design by Kirsty McManus

Editing by Serena Clarke

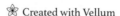 Created with Vellum

To my Mister Right
You accept me in all of my glorious imperfectness.
Thank you for your unfaltering belief in me.

ℭ

Keep in touch!

Want to stay updated? Subscribe to my newsletter at http://www.so-phieleighrobbins.com and claim a free short story, featuring the main character of The Best of You.

CONTENTS

CHAPTER ONE

DAY ONE: MIAMI

*A*nyone who assumes short people have it easy has clearly never been pushed against someone's smelly armpit while boarding a cruise. It was times like those I wished I'd been blessed with a couple of extra inches.

The queue at the dock snaked through the boarding area, swelling with every passing minute. Behind me, people started pushing into each other, as if that would make the line go any faster. All it did was force me to once again smell the sweaty senior invading my personal space.

I scrunched up my nose and put my carry-on bag in front of me. I hoped it would suffice as a barrier between me and the horrifying scent of salt and expired cheese wafting toward me.

I still couldn't believe I'd agreed to go on this cruise. I was a backpacker, a risktaker, a strong advocate of leaving the beaten track. And I disliked crowds with the intensity of an eleven on a scale of one to five.

Yet there I was, in the middle of a queue full of people who couldn't wait to board the Oceanic *Aphrodite* for a seven-day Caribbean cruise. As soon as I'd announced my cruise plans on my travel channel *That Backpacking Chick*, comments started pouring in. They ranged from surprised but encouraging to plain rude and utterly offensive. One person even accused me of being solely responsible for climate change and said she hoped I'd drown in the middle of the ocean.

That was the thing with having a popular travel vlog. Catering to almost one million followers meant that there was always someone who didn't like what I did, wore, ate or talked about.

In the beginning I would drive myself nuts trying to please them, but after a while I stopped trying to tick their boxes of approval and started to tick my own. It was one of the best decisions I could've made. Nowadays my number one advice for newbies in the vlogging field was *never read the comments*. Anyone who has an online presence knows the comment section is where vloggers' souls go to die a horrible death.

Smelly Senior made it to the front of the queue, and I prayed he would have the decency to jump straight into the shower as soon as he boarded the ship. If he didn't, then I felt sorry already for anyone coming into his pungent perimeter.

I was getting my own passport and camera out of my bag, ready to get on board as well, when I noticed some commotion going on behind me.

Still holding my camera, I stood on my tiptoes to see what was happening. A man was yelling, a child broke out in tears because of all the noise and then one of the luggage carts hit a woman, catapulting her to the floor. Ouch. That had to hurt. Luckily, someone rushed to her rescue.

I turned around again, now at the front of the line. A friendly crew member scanned my ticket and passport, handed me a folder with several documents, asked me some questions and snapped a pic, and sent me on my merry way with a big smile on his face.

As I walked over the ramp leading to the ship, I couldn't help but feel impressed. The ship seemed to go on and on in every direction. Rows of cabins lined the portside of the ship, as well as a bunch of big modern-looking lifeboats. They seemed safe, even though I hoped there wouldn't be a need for them. The last thing I wanted was to relive a disaster like Titanic, even if it meant meeting my own personal Jack Dawson.

A tall woman in a crew uniform greeted me at the entrance of the ship. "Hello and welcome aboard the Oceanic *Aphrodite*. We hope you'll have a wonderful time. And don't hesitate to talk to one of our many crew members if you have any questions whatsoever."

"Thanks, will do," I said and entered the massive ship.

I checked my papers again to see where my cabin was located. The ship was so huge that I would need a map to find the pool and the dining areas. It was such a stark contrast with the small hotels I liked to stay at and the old motorboats I loved to use for island hopping.

As I set foot into the atrium, I let out a gasp while I took in the scenery. The floors were made of actual marble, something I'd only expect to find in a fancy office building or a palace. Right in front of me was a double stairway with a golden chandelier dangling above it. To my left I spotted a statue of the Greek goddess Aphrodite.

I walked past the shops and restaurants toward the elevator, marveling at the enormity and beauty of the Aphrodite. As soon as I had unpacked everything, I would come back to explore.

After the elevator took me to the wrong deck twice I finally made it to room 7082, making sure to keep filming my every move. The cruise line had offered me a free upgrade to a deluxe ocean view cabin when I told them I'd be vlogging about my trip and would be sharing my findings with close to a million people. That was another thing I'd learned from vlogging. If you don't ask for it, no one is going to give it to you. But if you do ask...well, you just might find yourself in the VIP area of a cruise ship.

The only catch was that the last available deals for the cruise were part of a singles package, but I figured it wouldn't matter. No one could hold me down and force me to join a speed dating event or whatever activities people did on a singles cruise, now could they?

I pushed the door to my cabin open and let out a contented laugh. A nice-looking welcome package was sitting on a king-sized bed to my left. Right next to the balcony doors I spotted a sofa that housed a pull-out bed, and opposite that was a small desk. I could already see myself working there while stealing glimpses of the ocean and sipping a cocktail. Someone had placed my luggage neatly behind the bed. Wow. I could definitely get used to this level of service.

I heaved my suitcase onto the bed and started unpacking. I'd read online that you should bring twice the money and half the clothes when going on a cruise. Since I was short on cash, I'd brought twice the clothes and half the money.

When my clothes and toiletries were stored away, I checked the printed schedule. The ship wouldn't leave Miami Port until midafternoon, so there was plenty of time to explore the vessel before the mandatory muster drill.

With my camera around my neck, I headed to the elevators and traveled to the upper decks. The ship was unreal. Bars, restaurants, a pool, a casino, a spa... One of the decks even boasted a running track. Even if I wouldn't make it off the ship the entire week, I'd still have enough possibilities to keep me entertained.

After buying a Wi-Fi package, I decided to first record some footage on the lido deck, then order myself a drink from the Parnassus bar. Nothing screamed vacation like an ice-cold cocktail.

I walked around and made some panoramic shots of the entertainment areas before turning the camera to selfie mode.

"Isn't this amazing?" I said, speaking straight into the camera.

I always talked to my followers out loud, even in public places. It helped me connect with my audience. And what was the point of vlogging if you never uttered a word or were afraid of showing your face on camera?

"If you think hell is amazing, then yes, this is amazing."

Huh. That was definitely a first. Normally when I talked into the camera people looked at me as if I was nuts, but no one had ever shown the bravery to make a remark about it. Not out loud anyway.

I paused my recording and spun around to check out the grumpy specimen who couldn't contain himself from commenting on my non-question to him. But as soon as my eyes landed on this stranger's face, my irritation made way for surprise.

Leaning against a pillar was the most gorgeous guy I'd ever laid eyes on. His dark hair, long overdue for a haircut, made his green eyes pop and his strong jaw sported thick stubble. His shirt must've been made by a fashion god because it fit him in all the right places. If I were to look up *handsome man* in the dictionary, I was sure his picture would pop up. Not that his looks mattered – a man was the last thing I needed in my life. But I could still admire nature's best efforts, right?

"You think this place has a hell-vibe to it?" I asked.

He shrugged. "Lots of people packed together, too hot, no escape, plastic sandals and white polo shirts. Hellish."

"I think there's nothing wrong with this place," I said.

He cocked an eyebrow and nudged his head in the direction of a vending machine, the words *Lady Fortuna* flickering in neon lighting at the top.

"A dollar to get your fortune read by an old doll? I mean, come on, that's not quite heaven either."

"I'm sure if you put a dollar in, your message would be not to take life too seriously," I said.

"Maybe. I do regret making this cruise a part of my life though."

"Because you're shoeless?" I asked, pointing out the strange fact that he was barefoot.

He smiled at my question. "Amongst other things, yes. What's your name?"

"I'm Holly."

"Noah. Nice to meet you."

He put his arms on the railing and glanced at me sideways. "Do you always talk to yourself in public?"

"I do when it's for work," I said.

"That's good. For a moment, I was afraid you might be one of those crazy chicks. That's the last thing I need at the moment. Or any moment really."

"Well, Noah, I can confirm that I'm not crazy at all."

He laughed. "Isn't that exactly what a crazy person would say?"

"I guess you'll have to take my word for it."

He smiled at me. "I guess."

"You know what? You seem bummed out. Maybe you don't like vast spaces of open water or someone stole your shoes or you think the buffet looks nothing like the one they promised you in the brochure. Whatever is bothering you, I'm sure it's fixable. And just to prove to you that the future is indeed bright, I'm going to put a dollar into this tacky machine and have your fortune read."

I walked over to the vending machine and slid a dollar into the money slot. Noah joined me. He threw me a smile that reached all the way up to his eyes. Talk about nature's top achievements.

The machine whirred to life and the doll inside of it started to move in a robotic way. I glanced over at him and we both burst out laughing.

A small piece of paper fell out of the machine. I picked it up, reading the words out loud.

> *A life-changing event is going to turn your world upside down. Now is not the time to doubt yourself, now is the time to act. Make sure to keep your eyes and ears open for signs of unexpected opportunities.*

"So, what do you think?" I asked, handing him the slip of paper.

"Let's say I'm glad it wasn't one of my dollars that got wasted on this fake thing," Noah said with a grin on his face.

"It does sound generic, doesn't it?"

He nodded. That was probably my cue to leave, but I didn't feel like saying goodbye yet. Who knew when I would see Noah again? On a ship of thousands, it seemed unlikely that I would run into him any time soon.

It was now or never. If I wanted to spend more time with him, I'd have to be bold. Like the fortune doll said, *now is the time to act*. I didn't know why I wanted to be close to him, but I did. And who was I to go against something as honest as a gut feeling? Spending time with him would beat wandering around alone and having to think about my worries back home.

"Do you want to grab a cocktail with me?" I offered. "I was heading to the Parnassus bar."

"Sure, why not? But I think I need some shoes first."

"Right, the shoes. You've sure got me intrigued as to why you're running around like that."

Noah laughed. "It's not as exciting as you might think. My father took them after we had a small argument. God knows what he did with them. Probably chucked them overboard."

"Poor fish," I said with a laugh.

"Yeah, definitely. You know what? Let's skip the shoe shop and get that cocktail. There are weirder things than walking around shoeless on a cruise ship and it's not like I have to be anywhere any time soon."

We walked to the bar, found ourselves a table and ordered two piña coladas. It was weird how smoothly our conversation flowed, considering an hour ago I didn't even know he existed.

"Can I ask why you are on a cruise when you think this is a hellish place?" I asked, sipping my cold drink.

Noah played with the straw of his cocktail and sighed. "It's my own fault, really. You see, my dad's been alone for years now and he's only in his fifties. That's way too young to spend the rest of his life alone. I told him he needed to get out there and take a chance on love. I'm pretty sure that's what my mother would've wanted, for him to be happy again."

"Wanted?"

Noah nodded. "It's been seven years this spring."

"That must've been hard on you."

"It was. I mean, it still is and I miss her every day, but the sharp pain of it becomes a bit less every day as well. She had a great life and she really lived it, you know? No regrets, that kind of thing. Anyway, when I suggested this cruise to my father, he said the only way I would get him to agree would be to come with him. And that's how I find myself on a singles cruise to the ˖h is completely out of character for me, believe

as well."

"Oh, yeah? So what brings you here then?"

"Work. If I can get my vlogging channel up to one million followers, a popular brand of outdoorsy equipment called Big Bear Co. is going to sponsor my episodes and I won't have to do odd jobs anymore to make ends meet. It's the first time I've been on a cruise, actually. I normally go backpacking without any solid plans."

All of that was true, but I didn't feel like telling him I had another reason for being on this cruise and that I'd only booked it last minute. I would get my channel to one million followers regardless of the cruise, but it was all too personal to tell a stranger. Besides, the less I had to think about the whole drama I'd left behind, the better.

Noah grinned. "So we're both here for reasons that have nothing to do with the scope of this cruise?"

I laughed. "I guess so, yes. Isn't that ironic?"

"Can't argue with that," Noah said.

"I'm sorry to interrupt," a blonde woman wearing a crew uniform said, handing us both a pamphlet. "I'm Lauren, part of the entertainment team, and I've got an exciting proposal for you."

"Let's hear it," Noah said, folding his hands behind his head.

"You two seem like people who love to have some fun, am I right?" she beamed. Without waiting for an answer, she continued, "There's a game night tonight right next to the amphitheater. Would you two want to form a team and compete? Every contestant gets a voucher for free drinks worth fifty dollars and the winners get a free excursion at one of our stops. There's also a small surprise included."

"Yes, we would," I said without thinking it through, even though Noah's eye rolling was making it absolutely clear he had no intention of agreeing to Lauren's proposal.

"What my friend here means is, no we don't," Noah said. "Sorry, I hate surprises."

I leaned in toward him. "Come on, it could be fun. Let's make the best of this cruise and try out all the silly things this ship has to offer. And if you hate it, you can always use your voucher afterwards and get drunk for free. We might even win."

He groaned. "I don't care about the free drinks. Can't we get crazy in other ways?"

"Come on, come on, come on, pretty please," I coaxed. "If you say yes, you get to choose something I have to do this week."

A mischievous grin spread across his face. "Anything?"

"Well, within the bounds of acceptable. I'm not eating spiders for your pleasure."

Noah laughed and extended his hand.

"Deal," he said. When our hands touched, a rush of excitement went through me. This was turning out to be a much more interesting cruise experience than I could've ever imagined.

CHAPTER TWO

*a*fter the mandatory muster drill, Noah and I parted ways and I returned to my room to get ready for the trivia night.

I took off my clothes and stepped into the tiny shower, then squeezed a dot of shampoo in my hands. While I was lathering my hair, I wondered if going to an event with a guy I didn't know all that well had been a good choice. Granted, Noah wasn't a complete stranger, but we had only spent half a day together. What if he turned out to be some sort of creep? I hadn't even met this alleged father of his. It could be a ploy to make him seem innocent.

Still, he seemed harmless and having a friend on this ship would be a nice surprise. If I spent all of my time alone my mind would try to find a way to remind me of the mess that awaited me back home. I could use a friend like Noah.

I toweled myself dry, got dressed and checked the messages on my phone. Three missed calls, all from this morning. I knew what they were about, but I didn't want to deal with them. Besides, what would I be able to do about it in the middle of the ocean? Jump in a lifeboat and paddle back to shore?

I switched my phone off and slid it in my bag. I had an exciting night planned and didn't care for any interruptions, especially not from *him*.

I closed the cabin door after one last check in the mirror, then rode the elevator to the lower decks.

The venue was buzzing with people by the time I arrived. I found a table in the back and ordered a glass of wine to ease my nerves. When I agreed to participate, I'd assumed everyone would be at the opening night in the nearby amphitheater, but apparently I had completely misjudged the situation.

A little before eight, Noah walked toward my table, an older man wearing a life vest in tow.

"You'll have to excuse my father. He thinks he needs to wear his life vest all of the time," Noah said as he took a seat next to me.

"I'll take it off when I go to bed, so technically I'm not wearing it all the time," his dad replied before turning his attention to me. "Hi there. I'm Robert, Noah's father."

"I'm Holly. Nice to meet you, Robert," I said.

"Do you think I look ridiculous? Be honest."

I shook my head. "Better safe than sorry, right?"

"Absolutely," Robert said. "I don't want to end up as fish food if this ship sinks, but Noah thinks I won't be able to find a woman if I keep walking around like this."

"I'm sure you will be able to meet someone regardless. You want a woman who loves the real you, right? Uncommon choices of clothing and everything."

Robert's face lit up and he threw Noah an *I told you so* smile. "See? This girl knows what she's talking about, son."

The emcee tapped the microphone and the chattering and laughing in the room faded away. It was time to get serious.

"Welcome to the first night of this cruise, ladies and gentlemen. Our contestants are waiting to get to the stage and they're bursting with enthusiasm. I would be too in their shoes, because the two winners will get the chance to be extras in Evan Parker's new video clip. Filming starts tomorrow morning before sunset and of course the lucky winners will also get to meet the man in person and snap a picture with him."

I clapped my hands together and elbowed Noah. "We get to be extras in Evan Parker's video clip? How awesome is this cruise turning out?"

Noah ran his hand through his hair. "Don't get your hopes up, we haven't won yet. And also, I don't know who this Evan Parker guy is."

I narrowed my eyes. "You don't? What about his hit song *Nothing Like This*?"

Noah shrugged. "Can't say that it rings a bell."

"I've known love before but it was nothing like this," I sang.

All I got in return was a blank stare. He really didn't know who Evan Parker was? What rock had he been living under?

"Noah doesn't keep up with the latest trends. That's what you get when you live on a deserted island," Robert chimed in.

Noah lived on an island? So many questions came bubbling to the surface, but I didn't have time to address them because all contestants were called to the stage. I shoved my camera into Robert's hands, hoping that he wasn't one of those tech-hating seniors.

"Will you film us while we're on stage? Just push this button once and you're good to go."

Robert turned the camera around in his hands as if it was some sort of exotic fruit, then told me he'd take care of it. I made sure the camera wasn't set to selfie mode anymore and made my way to the stage, where Noah and I took a seat together with six others.

The emcee tapped his microphone again. "Welcome every-one. My name is Max and right next to me we have our first contestant." Then he addressed Noah. "Would you mind telling the audience your name and why they should vote for you?"

Noah frowned. "To be honest, my friend here convinced me to enter. And my name's Noah."

"So you're both looking for love?"

Max held his microphone in front of my face and I blinked. "Love?"

"Yes, love. Legend has it that everyone who boards the *Aphrodite* will find true love. This is a dating show after all."

I gasped and shot Max an apologetic smile. "I'm sorry, but we were told this was a trivia night. You know, answering questions about trivial things?"

Max covered his microphone with his hand and whispered, "The trivia night is next door."

Next to me, Noah groaned. All color had left his cheeks and he threw me an angry look.

"So this is really a dating show? I didn't agree to that," he said.

"I'm sorry about the mix-up, but I'd love it if you considered staying. If my boss finds out that we made a mistake like this, he'll kill me," Max said in a pleading voice.

"I'm not interested." Noah clenched his jaw and got up, ready to walk away.

I grabbed his arm and pulled him back into his seat. "Please, Noah, don't leave me on this stage alone. Let's just win this. The two of us, okay? Quick, give me some facts about you."

"Are you nuts? I barely agreed to the trivia night, let alone some stupid dating show. I don't need to be matched to anyone. I'm happy being single."

"I hear you, loud and clear. Believe me when I say that I'm not looking for love either. But if we make sure we're matched together then it's a win-win for us. We get to be in that video clip and people will leave us alone for the rest of the cruise, thinking we've hit it off."

He crossed his arms. "Fine. But if we win, you're going stingray swimming with me."

I gasped. "I'm terrified of stingrays."

Noah uncrossed his arms and got up.

"Fine," I whispered. "I'll do it. Now sit back down. Please."

Max shot us a thankful look and Noah and I quickly exchanged some basics, like our favorite activity on a date and whether we would call ourselves a night person or a morning one, before the men got whisked away to the other side of the stage.

"Are you ready?" Max yelled. The audience started cheering and whistling in response.

I wanted to make the best of this experience. How much could go wrong?

𝄢

It turned out the answer to that question was *a lot*. Instead of answering a string of silly questions like they do in those blind date shows, we were presented with different challenges. Like trying to eat an apple with our hands tied behind our backs and doing an improvised scarf dance.

Every fifteen minutes, someone got voted off the stage by the audience. Noah was the last remaining guy and his expression didn't bode well.

"Hellish," he mouthed at me from across the stage. Gosh, he was definitely going to kill me later.

To make matters worse, I had to physically compete with an athletic blonde to be matched to Noah. All because he had answered one of his questions with a whole spiel about how much he appreciated a sporty girl.

"Wow, girls, the rope skipping went great, but how about some push-ups next? Whoever lasts the longest gets the guy," Max said while wiggling his eyebrows. The audience cheered and whistled. Too bad I didn't share their enthusiasm.

There was no way I would be able to win this challenge. Not that I didn't have a sporty bone in my body, I did like to run sometimes. But doing push-ups? They reminded me of my high school P.E. classes and not in a good way.

"Let's get down, ladies," Max shouted.

The other remaining girl and I positioned ourselves on the stage and waited for Max's signal to start.

Noah's expression transformed from grumpy to happy, almost as if he enjoyed seeing me suffer. I couldn't blame him though. I had been the one to get us both into this mess to begin with.

The other contestant started to push her arms up and down in a tempo that wasn't humanlike. And instead of calming down, she only seemed to accelerate. About two minutes in I was about to faint.

I could feel the muscles in my arms shake. It was only a matter of seconds before I would collapse. Noah clearly picked up on my desperate thoughts, because his expression clouded.

He had specifically told me earlier that he had no interest in dating anyone and now he was about to end up on a date with some random girl. Against his will. I couldn't do that to him.

I willed my body to cooperate, but it was no use. After five more push-ups, I collapsed onto the stage, the sweat running down my back and between my breasts. It was so not how I had envisioned the night would go.

The words of my ex had never rung truer: that I had a knack for getting into the most complicated situations.

I got up and was guided back to my seat by an assistant, leaving Noah all alone on the stage with Miss Muscle.

A dash of disappointment ran through me. It wasn't like I wanted Noah to like me in a romantic way. I didn't have the energy to let a man into my life again after what I'd just been through, but I'd at least hoped for a friendship.

"I need a cocktail," I said as soon as I was safely back in my seat, more to myself than anyone else.

"Now that's what I call entertainment. You killed it out there," Robert said, handing me a couple of tissues like a real gentleman.

I dabbed my face dry with them. "Noah's going to kill me. He doesn't want to get involved with anyone. He specifically told me he wants to be left alone this week and now I've set him up with this random woman who, for some unexplainable reason, is freakishly strong."

Robert shrugged and patted my sweaty arm. "Noah doesn't know what's good for him. He can't keep sulking forever about what happened on his wedding day. Or at least, what was supposed to be his wedding day. Heck, he even forced me to go on this cruise to meet someone new after my wife died. His story isn't even half as bad as mine and yet here I am, trying to seize the day."

Huh. Noah had been engaged? I should've known. A man like him, still single... It didn't add up unless something had happened.

"There you go." One of the waitresses had materialized at our table and put two frozen margaritas down in front of Robert and me.

"I don't think these are for us," I said.

"Courtesy of the gentleman over there," she said with a wink before disappearing into the crowd again. A few tables ahead of me I spotted one of the other contestants called Logan waving at me. I politely waved back before staring into my drink. *Please, don't let him come over here.*

"These are superb," Robert said. He took a big gulp, then patted his mouth with a napkin. "Do you know what's in them?"

"You've never had a frozen margarita before?"

"Not that I can remember."

"Tequila, lime juice, triple sec and agave syrup," I heard a woman say. "They're tasty, but far from healthy."

Noah stood right next to me, Miss Muscle stuck to his arm.

"Holly, Dad, this is Trina. She won me with her push-ups."

Trina started laughing like a maniac and patted Noah's arm. "Oh, stop it. I'm sure it was more than the push-ups."

"No," Noah mouthed at me. I couldn't help myself from giggling.

"This has been fun, but you'll have to excuse me, Trina. My father here needs to get back to his room. It's getting late and he needs his sleep."

Robert shook his head. "What are you talking about? I'm not ready for bed. Besides, I'm enjoying this frozen margertite, or what's it called."

"Margarita," Trina said, with a proud smile. "I know, because I go to Cancún every year. That's in Mexico. Have any of you ever been to Mexico?"

"I have," I said. "I even got caught up in a cartel fight there once. I only just made it out alive."

"Really?" Trina looked at me with eyes full of disbelief.

"Crazy, huh." So what if it wasn't one hundred percent true? It had really happened, only I was soaking up the sun at the hostel's pool when the bullets started flying two blocks away. I couldn't leave the hostel grounds for twenty-four hours and they ran out of chocolate bars just hours after the incident.

"What about you, Trina? Any exciting Mexican adventures you want to tell us about?" Robert asked.

Noah slumped down in his seat and Trina jumped on his

lap. No matter how funny that looked from where I was sitting, I had to do something to help him.

"Noah, remember how you told me earlier you were going to help me with some work stuff? Yeah, I forgot to mention it would have to be tonight. I'm on a deadline."

"Oh, yes, I remember. Now is the time to act, right?"

I nodded and turned my attention to Trina. "I'm sorry, but I have to whisk Noah here away. I would've loved to hear your stories, but we're needed elsewhere."

Noah alternated his gaze between his dad and Trina, concern written all over his face. "Are you going to be alright here?"

"Sure. You two go. Having a good work ethic is important," Robert answered, taking another sip of his cocktail.

Trina stood up from Noah's lap, looking disappointed that he was leaving her. "Are you sure you can't stay?"

"We really can't, sorry," Noah said.

Noah and I made our way to the exit, Noah a tad faster than I. If I didn't know better, I'd have thought he was running from a bloodthirsty tiger.

"Wait up," I said, trying to match his step.

"I'll see you tomorrow morning for our date," Trina called after him. "Don't be late."

As soon as the doors closed behind us, we burst out laughing.

"You're not mad anymore?" I asked.

"Oh, believe me, I will have my sweet revenge when we go stingray swimming. I'll even have you touch one of those suckers."

The doors opened again, and I saw Logan scanning the busy hallway.

"Should we keep running?" Noah asked, motioning toward Logan.

"I think so."

He grabbed my hand and pulled me into the nearest elevator. "Where to?"

"Let's just push a button and see where we end up."

"Let's."

I pushed one of the buttons and looked up at Noah to see him grinning at me with the most beautiful smile ever. Damn, those eyes were going to kill me if I wasn't careful.

CHAPTER THREE

DAY TWO: AT SEA

The phone in my cabin woke me from a restless dream. I peeled my eyes open and swallowed. Ugh. I needed water. Lots of it.

I stumbled toward the mini fridge and emptied half a bottle of water into the desert that was my mouth before the phone started ringing again.

One glance at the wall-mounted clock told me it was only five thirty in the morning. Who on earth could possibly need me at this hour?

"Hello," I said with a croaky voice.

"Good morning, sunshine."

"Noah? How can you be so chipper at this hour? And after barely no sleep?"

"The filming for Evan Parker's video clip starts in half an hour."

"I know, don't remind me. I hate that I have to miss it. Are you calling me to rub my nose in it?"

Noah snorted. "Let's say that Trina has canceled on me and that I get to take someone else. I could ask my father, but..."

"No, don't ask Robert. I'll be at your room in fifteen minutes. Seven triple one, right?"

"Great, I'll see you in fifteen."

I disconnected the call and started running around my cabin like a maniac. I was going to meet Evan Parker! Should I take a shower or pick out my clothes first? Was my camera charged? How about a quick cup of coffee?

Forcing myself to take five deep breaths helped to lift the clouds in my head. I plugged in my camera, figuring that fifteen minutes of charging was better than nothing, then hopped into the shower with my toothbrush. Multitasking wasn't always effective, but it was at moments like these.

Exactly fourteen minutes later, I knocked on Noah's door.

He joined me in the hallway, wearing jeans and a black fitted shirt. He looked as if he'd had at least eight hours of sleep, even though we had stayed in the Dionysus wine bar until three a.m. I on the other hand looked like a sleep-deprived junkie. Life wasn't fair.

"What happened with Trina? Last night she couldn't get enough of you," I said while we walked toward the elevator.

"You won't believe me if I told you."

"Try me," I said.

The doors to the elevator opened and I pushed the button for the lido deck. Noah leaned himself against one of the walls and ran a hand through his hair.

"Apparently she likes older men. Older as in, my father's age."

I laughed. "Noooo, really?"

"Turns out Dad loved her stories about Mexico so much that it sparked something in him. He only returned to our room an hour ago."

"Oh, no. They didn't..."

Noah shook his head. "I don't think they actually slept

together, thank goodness. But I'm happy my father is happy. Honestly, I don't mind him hooking up with Trina, even though it's weird. Don't you think it's weird?"

I bit my bottom lip. "It is a bit weird, yeah. But then again, is anyone ever completely normal?"

"Good point," Noah said. "You sure aren't."

"Hey, watch it," I said and punched him in the arm.

He pretended to be in pain and rubbed his bicep. "I just love messing with you."

We locked eyes and something stirred inside of me. I searched his face for a clue about what he was thinking, but couldn't find an answer.

Right on cue, the elevator pinged and the doors opened at the lido deck where we were greeted by a broad-shouldered guy in a security uniform holding a clipboard. Behind him the deck had been closed off with stanchions, and a small crowd of women was gathered at the side, unable to get through.

"Joining or watching?" he asked us.

"Joining. We won our spot during the show yesterday. The name's Noah Hunter. And this is Trina."

I shot Noah a look. Did he really just call me Trina? I almost scolded him, but then realized he'd had no time to swap her name on that list with mine.

The security guy scanned his list of names and let us through with a short nod. "Patricia over there will take care of you. Have fun."

This was so exciting. I had discovered Evan Parker's music five years ago and constantly listened to his songs on Spotify. That I got to be part of a video clip he was shooting and get a picture with him was more than I'd ever could've imagined.

Evan Parker was the epitome of a rock star, the kind of guy that makes all the other ones look like a cliché. Dark and brooding with badass clothes, a couple of tattoos, and a jawline that framed his face in the most beautiful way. The kind of unattainable dream guy that leaves women swooning wherever he went, including me.

"I'm so glad Trina decided to spend the night with your dad," I said with a sigh.

"You are? That's not creepy at all."

"Oh, stop it, you know what I mean. If Trina hadn't hooked up with your dad, I wouldn't have been able to experience this." I motioned to the set as if it was a slice of heaven.

Noah grinned at me, but didn't utter a word.

"What?" I asked.

"Nothing. Your enthusiasm is adorable."

Noah had somehow inched closer and as I looked up, I could see the details in his irises. Green swirled around in mesmerizing patterns. An involuntary sigh escaped my mouth. I followed up with a fake cough. I didn't want Noah thinking I was swooning over his eyes, even though I was.

At six o'clock sharp, Patricia introduced herself and addressed all of us.

"We're going to shoot a short sequence that will be used at the end of the video clip. Please, may I ask you to listen carefully to all the rules and instructions. We can only keep this deck closed off from other passengers for a short amount of time, so your cooperation is appreciated. Also, there's no filming allowed whatsoever," she said, looking me straight in the eye.

I sighed and lowered my camera. I should've known. Thank goodness I would be able to get a picture with Evan later on.

Patricia led us to a big open space on the deck that had been turned into a party zone for the recording. Brightly colored umbrellas and lounge chairs with towels draped over them were positioned around a cocktail bar.

"Everyone, grab a drink and position yourself on one of the

markers that you can see on the floor. Don't step too far away from your designated dance spot. And don't forget to smile."

Noah and I grabbed ourselves a beer bottle each and walked toward the front of the deck.

"We're nailing this," he said. "We're going to be the best fake party people ever. Deal?"

I laughed. "Sure, we can do that."

It took about eight takes before the director was happy and we could move on to the next shot. Shooting a video clip was more intense than I'd figured, but we did have a lot of fun. Noah kept doing the craziest moves, which made me laugh every single time.

Fifteen minutes later, Patricia stepped to the forefront again. "For the last shot, we'll need you guys to dance, count to ten, then hug someone close to you. The song is called *Love at Sunrise* after all."

Hug each other? Wouldn't that be awkward? I loved hanging out with Noah and staring into his beautiful eyes, but I'd only met him the day before. The small crowd that was watching the recording only added to my nerves, but I couldn't exactly back out either.

"Alright, people, let's go! The sun is almost too bright to get a good shot, so we need to act fast."

"You know what I'd like to know?" a girl to my left asked. "Where's Evan Parker? Why are we doing all the work without him?"

Patricia put her hand on her hip and cocked an eyebrow. "Dancing for an hour doesn't exactly mean you're doing all the work. Evan's been shooting all night and will be here soon, don't worry."

She walked away rolling her eyes and muttering something about stuck-up people. I knew how she felt, thanks to my vlogging channel. No matter what you did, there would always be someone who wasn't happy about it.

"And make sure to smile when you're hugging. It needs to look convincing, not like you've just been diagnosed with mad cow disease," Patricia shouted from the side of the deck.

"I don't even know what kind of look that is," Noah laughed.

"I'm guessing something like this," I said and pulled a funny face.

"You're crazy, you know that?"

I did a small twirl and bowed. "Thank you. Crazy and adorable, that sums it up right."

As Patricia called *action*, we started dancing and counting to ten. Nerves rushed through me when it was time to pull Noah in for a hug. As I held him close to me, I was amazed by how he felt. Soft, yet muscled. When Patricia let us do three more takes, I couldn't say I was disappointed.

"That's a wrap, people," Patricia shouted and everyone started cheering.

Those of us who had been able to secure a spot in the queue for a picture with Evan raced to the designated place.

With only three people in front of us, I shoved my camera in Noah's hands. "Here, will you make a short recording of me when I meet Evan? I know it's not allowed, but I need it for my vlog."

"What if someone sees me doing it and they confiscate your camera?"

I let out a laugh. "Confiscate? It's not like we're offering Evan a drug deal. It's harmless. Please?"

Noah shook his head. "You're going to be the death of me."

"Just hold it close to your pocket so you can shove it back inside if necessary," I said. "It doesn't matter if the images are shaky, as long as I can show something on my vlog."

Before Noah could protest, I was called to the front to meet

Evan. He looked even more gorgeous in real life than on television. I handed my phone to one of his assistants who was in charge of snapping the pics.

"Hey there, how are you today? Thank you for starring in my video," he said and smiled at me, then put his arm around me for a picture.

"Thank you for making such awesome music. I talk about your songs a lot on my travel channel called *That Backpacking Chick*," I blurted out. Noah had been right all along. I *was* crazy. What kind of thing was that to say to a famous rock star? My travel channel? Ugh.

Evan Parker didn't seem to mind though, because he smiled at me and then someone led me away before I could utter another ridiculous thing.

All in all, it was over before I could blink. I opened the Instagram app on my phone and posted the picture of Evan and me on my profile, promising to have the video with real-life footage of him up soon. It wasn't a case of arrogantly tooting my own horn. I did it because I knew it worked and I needed to up my following, even though I was over the moon that I got to meet Evan Parker.

Out of the corner of my eye, I saw Patricia walking over to me with fast strides. Crap. She probably got wind of my secret filming plans.

"Is there a problem?" I asked, giving her my most innocent smile while hoping she couldn't see my shaking hands.

"No, that's not it. I couldn't help but hear you say you're the owner of *That Backpacking Chick*. I just wanted to tell you that I love your channel."

"Oh, that's kind of you, thank you."

"Here's my business card. You never know what opportunities will come up." She smiled at me and walked away again.

It felt nice to be recognized. Not because I loved being in the spotlight, but because it meant my work was important to some-one. That validation was everything to me.

"Did you do it?" I asked Noah as he handed my camera back.

"I think so, although it's quite possible I've only filmed the inside of my pants."

"I'm sure there'll be a shot or two on there that I can use. So, what's next?"

"Breakfast, for sure. I'm starving," Noah said and we made our way to the dining room together.

Noah had promised to meet his father there and honestly, a big plate of food and a steaming cup of coffee was all I could think about in that moment.

Walking in, I immediately spotted Robert, which wasn't hard to do. Wearing a life vest nonstop has its perks after all, like being the center of attention wherever you go.

I went straight for the buffet, which was filled with yummy-looking food and juices. I grabbed a plate and filled it with eggs, toast, a bowl of fresh fruit and a breakfast muffin, then took a seat at Robert's table.

"Good morning," I said.

Seated next to Robert were three people I didn't know and, who else, Trina. She couldn't keep her hands off of Robert and laughed too loud at his jokes, which to be honest weren't even that funny. *Awkward.*

Next to Trina sat Mindy, a palm reader from Palm Springs who insisted on reading Noah's hand later. Whatever was wrong with my hands, I didn't know, but she didn't offer me a reading. Maybe because I had boobs and Noah didn't?

The grey-haired couple next to Mindy each shook my hand politely. "We're George and Georgia. We're newlyweds," the woman said, proudly showing us the rock on her finger.

"And you decided to spend your honeymoon on a singles cruise?" I asked.

"We're cruise experts. The themes don't matter to us; all we strive for is a badge of honor," George said.

"Honor?" Noah said, his lips twitching.

Georgia nodded. "That's right. This is our three hundred forty-eighth cruise. Two more and we'll get special recognition from the cruise line."

I made some quick calculations in my head. Three hundred forty-eight cruises, about seven days each, meant they'd already spent 2436 days of their lives on a cruise ship. Or almost seven years total. Wow. And people often called *me* nuts for traveling so much.

"We met on a cruise," George said. "Got married on one as well, two weeks ago. If there's anything, and I mean anything at all, you want to know about life on a cruise ship, you come to us."

"Well, do you have any recommendations for an excursion in Jamaica?" I asked, buttering a bread roll. "We dock there tomorrow and I haven't even thought about what to do once I get off the ship."

"Holly here is a travel blogger," Robert said.

"That's right, although technically it's called a vlogger."

Their blank stares urged me to explain myself.

"A blogger is someone who writes about certain topics online and a vlogger is someone who films themselves while doing stuff, then turns it into a nice video. In my case, it's all about traveling."

"Then you should definitely go white water rafting," said Georgia.

"Or go to the beach and try out the dive cliff."

"Oh, and do the zipline. Remember that one, George?"

It was like these people had been on every thrilling excursion there was, even though they looked no younger than sixty-five.

I made some notes in my phone so I could google the activities later on before deciding which one I was going to go with.

"Holly, I think someone is waving at you," Mindy said, pointing to the buffet.

"Yeah, don't look," Noah warned, but I couldn't contain the urge to look.

I turned around in my seat and looked straight at Logan. He was dressed in a white polo shirt and beige shorts, a salmon-colored pullover draped around his shoulders. Sandals and white socks completed his look. I cringed and tried to telepathically send him a message not to come over to our table, but Mindy waved back at him with enthusiasm.

"Don't encourage the guy," I whispered, but it was too late. Logan had clearly interpreted Mindy's waving as a sign that it was okay to approach our table. He walked toward us with confident strides. Maybe it wouldn't be so bad? The guy looked harmless enough and all he had done was buy me a cocktail the night before, which had in fact been a nice gesture.

"Good morning, Holly," he said, ignoring the rest of the table and wringing his hands.

"Hi there," I said.

"I was wondering, do you have any plans tomorrow? I'm all alone on this cruise and I'd love to go on a fun excursion, but I don't want to explore Jamaica on my own. Being alone in a foreign country usually upsets my bowels."

Wow, if that wasn't too much information, I didn't know what was.

"We're going white water rafting," Noah said.

I shot him the death stare. He shrugged and held up his hands. "Payback for yesterday," he whispered and patted my leg with the stupidest grin ever.

"That sounds wonderful. Meet you here at breakfast?" Logan asked and walked away before I could tell him no.

CHAPTER FOUR

*G*etting up early also meant getting a front seat at the pool. I needed some time alone to relax and think. I couldn't keep running from my worries forever.

I placed my bright yellow towel on one of the empty chairs, slipped my flats off and closed my eyes. The sun warmed my face and legs and after a few minutes, my muscles got more and more relaxed with every breath I took.

It had been ages since I'd been able to relax like this. I was always running around, editing videos, booking my next trip and – until recently – spending time with Kyle, my ex. At least I wouldn't have to invest another minute of my existence in him, now that he had removed himself from my life.

The image of him telling me we were over flashed before my eyes and I cringed. I still couldn't believe how he'd betrayed me. For the last two weeks, I'd been over and over it in my head and yet I couldn't think of a reason that justified what he'd done. I took care of the household chores, I always made sure he knew he was loved, I tagged along on group gatherings with his friends – even though I had nothing in common with them. I had promised to become his wife one day.

I thought we had a perfect thing going on, until Kyle announced that I would have to move out of our two-bedroom apartment because another girl was moving in. I'd struggled to find words after his statement. Was that what a punch in the gut felt like? Unexpected and painful?

I hoped he broke his legs while moving her stuff into what used to be *our* bedroom.

A tear rolled down my cheek. I quickly swiped it away. The pool wasn't exactly the most appropriate place to start bawling my eyes out over my miserable love life.

"Do you mind if I sit here?" a voice to my left asked.

I looked up. Logan stood next to an empty chair. He was wearing the same outfit as before, only now he had added a hat and a pair of sunglasses.

"Uhm..." I let the question hang between us. I hoped he'd see how upset I was and that I just wanted to be left alone for a while, but social cues didn't seem to affect him.

"The weather is great, isn't it? I assumed it would be too cold to hang out by the pool, but it turns out I was wrong." He checked an app on his phone and shoved it in my face. "See? Seventy-four degrees. How remarkable, right?"

"Sure," I said, even though I didn't know the first thing about the average temperature on a cruise like this.

Logan put down his towel on the beach chair and neatly tucked the corners in. Then he started lathering himself with SPF50. All in all, it took him about fifteen minutes before he was finally ready.

"You don't mind putting sun lotion on my back when my alarm goes off, do you? I need to switch sides every twenty minutes or I get burnt really bad, blisters and everything."

"I guess?" I replied.

I pulled my book out of my bag and flipped it open. Logan seemed like a nice guy, but I wasn't in the mood for small talk.

"What are you reading?" he asked, trying to look at the cover.

"It's a romance novel," I replied.

"Is it set in space? Me personally, I love space stories, especially Star Trek. I've even done a course in Klingon. Do you want me to say something in Klingon? Because I totally can."

Did I want him to speak Klingon to me? Was he being serious?

"I'm good, thanks," I said with a smile, which only spurred him on.

"NuqDaq 'oH tach'e'," he said. "It means 'where's the bar?'"

So he *was* being serious.

"That's great, Logan. Now, if you don't mind, I'm going to read for a bit."

"Sure, go ahead. Reading is amazing. I love how it transports you to other worlds, worlds that have completely different rules from ours. Take the world of Star Trek for example. Could you imagine ever living in a universe like that? Or being a crew member of the Starfleet?"

I arched my brow. He was never going to stop talking, was he?

One hour later, I was about to run away screaming. I'd listened to his Star Trek trivia, put sun lotion on his back and patiently answered all of his questions about being a vlogger.

But he just wouldn't stop. I hadn't been able to read one word of my novel or to even think for myself. He followed me around when I went for a refreshing swim in the pool and when ordering a smoothie at the pool bar. The moment he wanted to follow me into the ladies' bathroom, I freaked out.

Sitting on the toilet with Logan guarding the door against my will, I pulled my phone out of my bag and sent an SOS message to Noah. I didn't want to take up his time, but someone needed to come and rescue me before I shoved Logan overboard.

"Everything okay?" Logan asked. "I think those eggs this morning might not have been the best quality."

"No comment," I answered and trudged back to my seat.

By the time Noah arrived, Logan had circled back to his favorite topic ever: Star Trek. All iterations and specials.

"Heya," Noah said. "Are you ready?"

"I am." I jumped up, shoved my things into my bag and rolled my towel up.

"I'm sorry, Logan, but I'm going to steal her from you for the rest of the day."

"Oh, well, I guess I'll see you two tomorrow then. Unless whatever you've got planned today can include me?"

My heart went out to him. It couldn't be easy for him to feel this lonely. Or at least, that's what I assumed his desperate attempts meant. But I had to be firm with myself. I had this tendency of pushing my own needs to the background to help others, even when it wasn't a pleasant experience for me. I didn't go on this cruise to make others comfortable. For once, I needed to make myself comfortable.

"We'll see you tomorrow when we dock in Jamaica," I said and waved goodbye.

As soon as we were out of earshot, I let out a heavy sigh. "I'm so sorry, he just didn't want to stop talking. It was driving me crazy."

"I'm sure he would've stopped talking if you had asked him nicely. In Klingon of course," Noah said, the corners of his mouth lifting up.

"Gosh, don't remind me," I said, laughing.

Noah stopped in front of the cocktail bar. "I was about to sign up for the FlowRider. Do you want to join me? It's a surf simulator," he added when he saw my confused look.

"I'm not opposed to checking it out," I said.

We sat down in the seats opposite the FlowRider where a small crowd had gathered. A middle-aged man in blue swim briefs was trying to beat the waves, but he kept falling down.

When he was finally able to stand on the surfboard, he flexed his bicep with a grin on his face, then got swept away by the water. He tumbled down, made a head roll and landed in the water, flat on his belly. Ouch.

"That's my cue," Noah said and went to one of the crew members to sign a waiver. George and Georgia walked past and I waved them over.

"Noah's about to try the FlowRider," I said, pointing at him.

George turned his gaze's into Noah's direction. "What do you say, Georgia? Shall we watch the kid trying to catch a wave?"

She nodded in agreement and they settled down next to me, offering me a portion of their nachos. When I politely declined, Georgia elbowed me. "You don't want to smell like nachos when your man returns, am I right?"

I waved my hand at her and laughed. "Noah and I are just friends. He's not my man."

"I've seen the way he looks at you. There's something going on between you two and denying it doesn't make it less true," Georgia said with a wink. "Isn't that right, George?" Now he got elbowed by the feisty old lady.

"What?" he asked with a mouthful of nachos.

"Men." Georgia rolled her eyes, then planted a kiss on George's cheek. "Can't live with them, can't live without them."

I smiled in response and pondered her words for a moment. If it was true that she'd seen Noah looking at me in a certain way, did that mean he was attracted to me? Or was I simply giving Georgia's words too much weight?

"Oh, look, Noah's about to get on the surfboard," I said, straightening my back to get a better look at him.

He was chatting with the surf instructor. He'd taken off his shirt, revealing a tanned upper body that made me weak in the knees. If I hadn't been sitting down, I would've buckled for sure.

"Take a look at that body. Whether you admit liking him or not, you can't deny that he looks like a god," Georgia said.

Heat rose to my cheeks.

"I guess, if you look at it objectively."

She was absolutely right, though. His body moved fluently on the board. It was clear this wasn't his first time surfing. With every movement his muscles tensed in the most sensual way ever. The water slid down his body and dripped down into the flow of water beneath him. He looked so sexy that I felt my heart starting to pound a tad faster than usual.

I turned my camera on and shot Georgia a look before she could comment.

"This is for my vlog, no ulterior motives."

She threw me a warm smile. "Whatever you say, sweetie, I don't mind. But if I could give you one piece of advice?"

I nodded. "Sure."

"If you do have feelings for him, or anyone else for that matter, don't push them away or hide them. Life's too short to run away from love."

"Thanks, I'll keep that in mind."

She gave my leg a squeeze. I wondered how she had figured out I'd rather run from love than embrace it again.

Noah did some tricks, eliciting lots of cheers from the audience. Especially from the women. A twinge of jealousy hit me out of the blue, but I made sure to push it away as fast as possible. We were friends, end of story.

"That was a lot of fun. Do you want to try it?" Noah asked when he returned.

"I don't think I'll be able to stand up straight on that board.

How about we go and grab some gelato? You guys are welcome to join us," I told George and Georgia.

"You two go and have fun," Georgia said. "We're about to hit the spa for a couple's massage. But we'll catch up later for sure." The two of them waved us goodbye.

Noah and I made our way to the ice cream restaurant. I went for a cone with two scoops of strawberry and he chose two chocolate scoops.

"Do you want whipped cream on that?" the guy behind the counter asked.

"No, thanks."

"Come on, live a little, Holly. I'm even getting sprinkles on mine." Noah grinned at me and I couldn't help but get sucked in by his enthusiasm.

"Okay, I'll have whipped cream. And sprinkles please."

The guy handed us our orders and we made our way to one of the lounge areas. The vast ocean spread out all around us and the sun was shining bright.

"It's hard to believe how far away we are from land," I said, looking out at the blueness surrounding us.

"Being on the ocean does have its charms."

His comment reminded me of something I'd been meaning to ask him. "Your father said something about you living on an island. Is that true or was it some kind of metaphor?"

"It's true. During the winter months, I take care of a billionaire's private island. It's perfect for me. No people to nag me, I get to spend my days in nature and I get paid a year's salary even though I'm only there from October to the end of March. Not that I'm in it for the money," he quickly added.

He took care of a billionaire's island? What a lucky guy.

"You'll have to invite me over some day. I'd love to see what a billionaire's island looks like," I said.

Noah chuckled. "It's not that different from any other island, except maybe for the luxuries like a helipad and beach villa."

"You know how to fly a helicopter?" I practically shouted the words.

"Yeah, I do. What about you?"

He seemed to want to steer the conversation away from himself. I was intrigued as to why, but didn't press.

"I can hardly drive a car, let alone fly a helicopter," I said jokingly.

Noah gave me a playful push. "I mean, with your vlogging channel and stuff."

I told him all about how I'd gotten into the vlogging field after a trip to Asia one summer and how I'd managed to fund my trips before I started making any money from advertisements on my channel.

We segued into the topics of favorite holidays, funny travel experiences and travel bucket lists. Then we chatted our way through lunch without so much as a beat of silence between us.

After our meal together, we each went to our rooms and got changed out of our swimwear. We spent the afternoon weaving in and out of the onboard shops, then shared a sushi platter for dinner and went for a stroll on the deck. It was as if we'd been friends forever.

The cold air made me shiver and I rubbed my arms with my hands.

"Do you want to go inside?" Noah offered.

"Let's watch the sunset together first. I've never seen the sun set while in the middle of the ocean."

"Sure."

We both focused on the mesmerizing scene in front of us and as the sun set, Noah draped his sweater over my shoulders. When he also put his arm there to keep the sweater in place, I was sure this trip couldn't get any better.

For a moment, all of my troubles were pushed to the background and a feeling of bliss enveloped me.

I looked up at Noah and he smiled at me in response, making me feel as wobbly as a cup of jelly. And all I could think about in that moment was leaning in and kissing him.

CHAPTER FIVE

*T*rying to fall asleep was easier said than done. I couldn't get Noah out of my head. It had taken me every shred of strength not to act upon my instincts and make a move.

No matter how much I wanted to in that perfect moment, kissing him wouldn't have been right. I was still in a shambles after finding out Kyle had cheated on me. And Noah had issues of his own to work on, or at least that's what Robert had me believe.

But then why did I keep getting drawn to him like a magnet? Was it a case of misery loves company or was I just mesmerized by his charming nature, his looks and his humor?

I flipped the light switch on and got my phone from its place on the nightstand. The video I'd shot of Noah on his surfboard earlier that day made my heart do cartwheels. It made me want to find out more about him.

I opened my internet browser and let my fingers hover over the keyboard for a while, trying to decide what the right move was.

Then I typed in his name on Google. To my disappointment,

he didn't seem to be on social media, but I did find an article mentioning him. It dated back to the previous summer and was titled *Noah Hunter & Kate Wilson set to get married next spring*.

The picture accompanying the article showed Noah with a tall brunette. She looked straight into the camera, a big smile on her face and her fingers splayed apart, showing an enormous diamond ring. Her other hand was draped around Noah's neck.

I scrolled down and started reading.

Noah Hunter & Kate Wilson, daughter of billionaire CEO Charles Wilson, are engaged. They have planned a May wedding, which will take place on a private island in the Bahamas, according to the bride-to-be.

I closed the article and went over to Facebook. I popped Kate's name into the search bar, hoping she would have her profile set to public. It took me a while to find her, though. Kate Wilson turned out to be a popular name, so I had to scroll through dozens of unrelated profile pages first.

When I finally got to her page, I immediately went through her pictures. I stopped at a particular one posted just last month. Again, Kate was showing off a diamond ring, only it wasn't Noah who was hugging her, but a completely different guy.

The picture was captioned: *"I can't wait to spend the rest of my life with this man!"*, and it had gotten 147 lovely comments.

Poor Noah. He had been burned just as bad as I had, if not worse. His reasons for not wanting to date someone were probably the same as mine. To not get his heart broken again.

I put my phone back on the nightstand. Should I talk about any of this to Noah and tell him my own story as well? They do say that misery loves company. Or would it be better to pretend that I didn't know anything?

I wanted to tell him I understood completely. That I too didn't think I'd ever be able to trust anyone that much again. But I didn't want him to know I'd googled him either, and make things weird between us. It was wonderful to have a friend on board. I didn't want to do anything to jeopardize that. It would be better to keep my mouth shut, at least for now.

ⓒ

Day Three: Jamaica

Touching land again after two days at sea was liberating. The *Aphrodite* offered a lot of fun activities, but nothing beat exploring a new country.

Before we got off, we were told numerous times that we would have to be back in time or the ship would set sail without us. I set a timer so I wouldn't forget. Being left behind wasn't one of the thrilling experiences I was looking for.

Our group gathered at the pier where a guide was waiting to take us white water rafting.

"Welcome to Jamaica, everyone. My name is Bembe and I'll be your guide for today. Who's ready to have some fun?" he asked.

"I am," Trina called out and hooked her arm around Robert's.

I followed Noah and the rest of our group to the van that would bring us to the river. George and Georgia were going to explore the town and we promised to meet up with them for a cocktail on the beach after our excursion.

Logan hurried into the van and sat down beside me. Great.

When this cruise was over, I'd be an expert on everything Star Trek.

"Did you have a fun night? I didn't see you at dinner," he said.

"I shared a sushi platter with Noah last night. We thought it'd be fun to switch things up and not eat at the dining room every day."

His face fell at the mention of Noah.

"Are you two talking about me?" Noah plopped himself down in the seat behind us and leaned forward. "I hope it's nothing but good things."

"Maybe," I said with a grin.

As soon as Trina, Robert and five other cruise ship passengers had found themselves a seat, Bembe started the van and we drove off.

It was beautiful there. Green and sunny, two of my favorites. I closed my eyes for a second and took a deep breath. I was glad I'd come on this cruise and not just because it meant I could get away from Kyle.

We arrived at the river twenty minutes later and Bembe gave everyone a helmet and life vest, except for Robert who was already wearing one.

"As soon as you're ready, please gather round for the safety briefing."

"Is a helmet really necessary?" Trina asked. "It messes my hair up."

Bembe shrugged. "No helmet, no stepping into the boat."

Robert patted Trina's arm. "It's okay, honey, you'll look great regardless."

Noah and I exchanged a look.

"Honey?" I whispered.

Noah rolled his eyes. "I know. This is not what I had in mind when I talked to him about meeting someone new."

"It's also cute in a way, no?"

"If your definition of cute is your father asking you when would be an appropriate moment to dive under the covers with his thirty-five-years-younger holiday crush, then it's absolutely cute."

I scrunched my nose up. "He didn't."

"Believe me, I wish you were right."

I pressed a hand to my mouth to stifle my giggles.

"Oh, you think it's funny, do you? How about this? Do you think this is funny as well?"

Noah grabbed me by the waist and started tickling me all over.

"Stop, please, stop," I said with heaving breaths.

"I'm enjoying this way too much to stop."

Noah laughed and kept on tickling. I tackled him and we both fell onto the ground.

"Please, I can't take it anymore," I said, tears of laughter running down my face.

He pinned me down for a moment and dipped his gaze to me. Warmth spread across my chest, the heat from his touch burning my skin.

"Ahem."

I broke my gaze away from Noah to see everyone looking at us. Some more amused than others. Logan clenched his jaw and shot me a desperate look, almost as if I was cheating on him.

Noah jumped to his feet and pulled me up. I rubbed some sand off my legs, then put my helmet on. Bembe started his safety briefing, which prompted Robert to get a notebook and pen out of his backpack.

I elbowed Noah. "What is he doing? How is he even going to check his notes while paddling?"

He let out a chortle. "Guess we'll find out in a minute or two."

After the briefing, the group got divided in half. I got into a boat with Bembe, Noah, Logan, Trina and Robert. The others got into the second boat and were joined by another guide.

With a paddle in my hands, I was more than ready to enjoy the thrill of fast rapids and waterfalls, but as a boat full of children passed us, I wondered just how thrilling this ride was going to be.

"Let's get this baby moving," Bembe called out and we all paddled forward.

At first, there wasn't much to it, but after about five minutes, we approached the first twist. The water rushed around the boat. We had to paddle together to keep the front from turning in the wrong direction.

As we cascaded down the river, a gush of water sprayed into the boat.

"I'm wet." Trina's shriek made Bembe laugh.

"That's the whole point of this ride. The wetter, the better," he said.

We passed an old stone bridge and had to master another cascade. From there on, the river widened and deepened, and Bembe stopped the boat.

"You can swim here for a while, just make sure to stay at the sides so that you don't bump into other rafts."

I asked Bembe to snap some shots of our group with my camera and jumped into the water. I turned myself on my back and let myself float around. Green leaves hung over the river and sunlight filtered through them, warming my face.

Logan stayed near the raft, looking lost. I felt sorry for him. It was clear he wanted to hang out with me and I kept pushing him away. It's just that I wasn't comfortable with someone smothering me like that. Still, I wasn't the kind of girl who treated people badly, so I swam toward the raft to talk to him.

"It's nice out here, right?"

He immediately perked up. "Very. Have you been rafting before? It's my first time. I don't travel much."

"I've been white water rafting. The Magpie River in Canada is the best. I nearly peed myself because I'd never been on water that rough, but the scenery is stunning."

"I wish I could travel more often, but I don't like to go alone. Going on this cruise was a big step for me."

"You should check out my vlog. I've got an episode all about traveling solo."

"I might, although I'm not sure about traveling solo again. It can get pretty lonely."

"True, but there are lots of ways to avoid feeling lonely on a trip."

Logan winked, a grin on his face. "Like talking to pretty girls at the pool on a cruise ship?"

I frowned. "That's a bit specific, don't you think?"

"Yeah, but it does work."

Oh, man. He was flirting with me. He even thought it was working, when all I wanted was to be nice to him.

I threw him a closemouthed smile. "Maybe it works for some. It doesn't for most people, though."

Relief washed over me when Bembe called us back to the raft, and we continued our descent down the river. One hour later we were all wet and tired, but more than satisfied as well. It had been a fun trip so far and the day wasn't over yet.

I changed into a pair of dry clothes and posted a picture of the day's adventures while I waited for the rest of our group to get ready. As I scrolled through pictures tagged with #oceani-caphroditecruise, I came across a familiar face. Mine.

I clicked on the picture. There I was, in my bikini, floating down the river. What the hell? Panic rushed through me as I discovered it wasn't the first one of me. There were five others, most of them starring me in my swimwear.

As I examined the profile picture of the perv posting bikini pictures of me, the penny dropped. The profile belonged to Logan.

Noah appeared from the dressing cabin and I shoved my phone under his nose. "Look at this. What do I do with it? Logan posted these all over the internet."

"Wow, that's inappropriate. And you didn't know he was posting these?"

"I didn't even know he had taken them. And look at these captions. *Spending the day with her.* What's that supposed to mean?"

Noah bit his lip. "Do you want me to talk to him?"

I drew in a sharp breath. "I'll do it. But if you don't mind, I'd love some support."

"Of course."

We got up and waited for Logan to come out of the dressing cabin.

"Can we talk for a minute? It's important," I said, crossing my arms over my chest.

"Sure, what's up?"

I showed him the pictures I'd found on his profile. "This is what's up. I don't feel comfortable with you posting these."

Logan's face fell. "Oh, I didn't think you'd mind."

"Really?"

"You have a ton of followers. I didn't think it would be a problem for you to appear on the internet."

"My follower count is totally unrelated," I said, anger swelling in my chest. "You don't go posting bikini pictures of someone without asking their permission."

Logan said nothing, so I continued. "Would you please delete them?"

His eyes grew big. "Delete them? But then my friends will think I've made it all up."

Noah took a step forward. "Look, mate, she doesn't care what your friends think about these pictures. It's not appropriate and she's asking you nicely to delete them."

Logan glared at me without blinking. "I see what this is. I get it. You two are a thing, aren't you?" He turned his gaze to Noah. "And you're jealous because another man posts pictures of her."

Noah held his hands up. "Yeah, you got me. It's got nothing to do with respect, I'm just jealous."

Logan's nostrils flared. "I thought we had something special going on."

"Wait, what? What gave you that impression?"

He held his fingers up and ticked them off one by one. "For starters, we almost got matched during the first evening, that's got to mean something. Then you asked me on this excursion and we had a great time at the swimming pool yesterday. You even offered to put sun lotion on my back."

Wow, this guy had issues that were far worse than I'd imagined. And to think that I felt sorry for him earlier.

"Be honest, Holly. Is Noah your boyfriend? I need to know. If he is, then I won't continue pursuing you. If he's not, I think you owe me a fair chance to win you over. I won't stop until your heart belongs to me."

I threw Noah a panicked look. If I told Logan the truth, there was no way he was going to leave me alone, he'd said so himself. But if I lied, I would have to pretend to be Noah's girlfriend for the remainder of the cruise and I didn't want to get him involved.

Before I could decide what to say to Logan, Noah put his arm around my shoulders and smiled. "We wanted to keep it a secret, but yes, Holly and I are together. She's my girlfriend."

CHAPTER SIX

"What?" I blurted out.

"Don't worry, our secret was bound to come out sooner or later," Noah said and winked at me.

I swallowed and tried to compose myself. "Yes, you're right. I'm sorry, Logan, but my heart already belongs to someone and that person is Noah," I said, pulling him closer for good measure.

A disappointed look crossed Logan's face. "I appreciate your honesty. I do hope we can still be friends."

"Yeah, of course we can. But there's no need to keep... pursuing me."

"Just one tiny piece of advice though, Holly. Don't send out mixed signals about your intentions. Us guys have feelings too." He turned on his heel and walked away.

Noah raked a hand through his hair. "That didn't go as expected."

"What is he even talking about? I never sent out any signals to him whatsoever."

"Maybe Logan isn't good at deciphering women's signals. It's not an easy specialty."

I sighed. "I'm sorry for getting you involved in all of this."

"Don't worry about it."

"We don't have to keep it up, of course. I don't want you to feel pressured."

Noah took my hand in his, sending a warm feeling through me. "I don't trust this guy. I'm not saying he's going to harm you, but he's got boundary issues. If pretending to be your boyfriend will keep him away from you, then I don't mind at all. We were spending lots of time together already anyway. Plus, it'll be good for me as well. That Sassy Singles group keeps popping up all over the ship, trying to coax me into joining their activities. One of them propositioned me after breakfast this morning."

"So we're doing this?"

A mischievous look crossed his face. "We are. And I bet it's going to be a ton of fun."

"All aboard," Bembe called out, waiting by the open door of the van. Noah and I climbed in and took the seats at the back.

The ride to the beach was short, but not short enough for the others to start asking questions. Apparently Logan had let everyone know Noah and I were a thing.

"How amazing is this? Father and son both found love on the same cruise," Trina said while squeezing Robert's hand.

Robert on the other hand seemed suspicious, but his smile told me he was happy for us. "So the legend of finding love on the *Aphrodite* is true after all, huh. Who would've thought? Congratulations."

"Oh, I know, we could double date." Trina jumped up and down in her seat and clapped her hands together.

"Yeah, maybe," I said.

The van came to a halt and Logan got out as soon as Bembe opened the doors.

"Are you two joining us on the beach or do you have other plans?" I asked Robert and Trina.

"You bet," Trina said. "I've done enough physical activity for the day. I need a beach chair and a cocktail."

I scanned the beach and spotted George and Georgia waving at us.

"Great. Let's go."

I took off my shoes and we crossed the beach to join George and Georgia. The feeling of warm sand between my toes brought a smile to my face. Beaches were my happy place.

"Don't you just love the beach?" I looked at Noah, who smiled.

"I do, thank goodness, as I live on an island," he said.

"Right, I keep forgetting you have your own personal paradise."

"I'm sure your place isn't bad either," he offered.

A nagging feeling formed in the pit of my stomach. I did have a nice place, only it wasn't mine anymore. Kyle had made sure of that. Out with the old, in with the new. I let my mind wander to his new girlfriend sleeping in the bed we used to share, drinking from the mugs we bought together and using the throw pillows I'd picked out for the sofa.

I did consider taking everything with me so that they'd have to buy new furniture, but did I really want to sit on a couch they had sat on, doing... well, stuff I didn't want to think about.

Ugh. It was enough to make me hate her, even though I didn't have a clue who she was. I hadn't found the courage yet to look her up online. As long as I didn't know her, I could imagine she was a stupid, brainless, ugly girl. Maybe she looked like a troll. The real truth might be too much to handle, so I preferred believing in my own.

"I'm kind of between places at the moment," I said.

"Where are you moving to?"

I stopped walking and turned to Noah. Now that he was pretending to be my boyfriend, I had to be honest with him.

"It's a long story, but the guy I used to live with kicked me out."

He gave me a curious look. "Were you two roommates or were you involved?"

"He was my fiancé, and he left me for someone else. She's sleeping in the bed he and I used to share. I don't know what to do. He's been calling me nonstop since I got on this cruise. He wants to know when I'll pick up my stuff, but I have nowhere to go. I've been able to avoid his calls so far, but I'll have to talk to him eventually."

Tears sprang to my eyes and I took a deep breath to keep them from falling. If I let one out, dozens of others would follow suit, and I didn't want to have a crying fit in the middle of a Jamaican beach.

"Oh, Holly, that's horrible." Noah softly pulled me closer to him and as my head hit his shoulder, I couldn't keep the tears in any longer. He gently ran his hands over my back. If I'd known that having a good cry while being held by an amazing guy would make me feel better, I'd have done it much sooner.

"I'm sorry, I don't want to ruin our day at the beach."

"Hey now, it's fine. Believe me when I say that I know exactly how you feel."

"Ashamed?"

"Why would you feel ashamed? If anything, your ex should be the one who feels ashamed. Who does that? Kicking out the woman you promised to marry?" He pulled a paper tissue from his backpack and swept it across my face. "You know what they say? That living well is the best revenge. Why don't we try to have as much fun as possible this week? Don't let that guy stop you from living your life. You can't give him that satisfaction."

I swallowed. "You're right."

"Will you be okay? We could go back to the ship if you want to."

I shook my head. "A couple of hours at the beach will do me good. Thank you."

Noah took my hand in his and together we walked to the rest of the group. When we arrived, Georgia clapped her hands together.

"I knew you two were perfect for each other," she said. "This calls for a celebration."

"They serve cocktails straight from pineapples and coconuts here. Pure heaven," George chimed in.

"I wouldn't say no to a good piña colada," I said.

"Make that two." Noah spread out a towel on the sand and took his shirt off. I quickly averted my gaze before realizing that was a mistake. A real girlfriend wouldn't look away if her boyfriend showed his muscled chest.

"I want one as well," Trina said.

Noah looked around the group. "That's three votes for piña colada. Anyone else want something?"

"I do, but I want to have a look at the menu first. Holly, will you join me?" Georgia asked.

"Sure," I said. Together we strolled over to the beach bar.

"So? How did this happen all of a sudden?" she asked after placing our order.

For a minute I contemplated telling her the truth, then decided against it. It would be better if Noah and I were the only ones who knew the truth. I wouldn't want to risk Logan finding out we'd lied to him.

"I don't know, how do these things happen, right? But it's still early days. We're taking it easy," I said.

She wiggled her eyebrows at me. "If I were you, I don't think I'd be able to constrain myself to take it easy."

I let out a chuckle. "He does have a killer body, doesn't he?"

Georgia nodded. "And as far as I can tell, he has a golden heart as well."

"He really does."

She wasn't wrong. Noah had spent most of his time with me already, even though he could be doing other things on this cruise. He even helped me to get Logan to keep his distance. He truly had a heart of gold.

The bartender placed our drinks on a tray and we walked back to our spot on the beach.

"Make sure to cherish a man like that," Georgia said. "Once you've found true love, don't let it go or you'll regret it for the rest of your life."

"Thanks," I replied.

I wasn't planning on letting Noah go. Not in a romantic way of course, but as a friend. He was there for me, he made me laugh and... he made me feel safe.

"These taste as good as they look," Robert said, sipping his cocktail straight out of a halved pineapple.

Trina nodded. "Pure heaven."

"Here's to love," Georgia said, holding her coconut up.

Noah and I exchanged a look and we smiled at each other. It was fun to share a secret, just the two of us. It had this intimacy to it that I absolutely adored.

"To love."

⌒

We made it back to the ship by dinner time after what turned into a fun and refreshing beach day. I hadn't spotted Logan since our return from the river though. I hoped he was doing okay, even though I was still feeling creeped out by him posting those bikini pics of me. At least he had deleted the pictures as promised.

When we had all filled our plates with dessert, Mindy announced she was going to read Noah's palm. She claimed it was calling to her, and the rest of us were dying to find out what secrets or surprises she was about to uncover.

Noah put his fork down and offered his palm to Mindy. "Lay it on me. Except, don't tell me the bad stuff."

She was silent for a while, except for the occasional hum. I tried to peek over her shoulder to see what was so special about Noah's hands, but they looked pretty normal to me.

"Do you have any advice or insights for Noah?" Trina asked, breaking the silence.

"I do." Mindy looked Noah straight in the eye. "Don't be afraid to show your feelings. Express whatever is inside of you and follow your passions. I can tell you are being reluctant with opening yourself up. If you open your heart chakra, good things will come your way."

Noah frowned. "My heart chakra?"

"It needs healing. But don't worry. What is broken can be mended."

"Well, thanks for that, Mindy. I'll definitely work on that heart chakra."

She threw us an intense look. "I'm sure Holly can help you with that."

"Yeah, don't be afraid to show people that you are a couple," Trina said, who definitely didn't suffer from the same problem. She had practically crawled onto Robert's lap and couldn't stop giggling while feeding him chocolate cake.

Noah planted a kiss on my cheek and got up. "As much as I'd love to discuss my love life with all of you, Holly and I had a romantic evening planned."

"We'll see you at breakfast tomorrow." I followed Noah to the elevators.

"I'm sorry about that," he said. "I just didn't want them to push the subject. Next thing you know, they'll be demanding a public kissing scene from us."

"Yeah, imagine that," I said, stepping into the elevator.

"Trina does have a point, though. If we were a real couple, we'd be all over each other. We should at least hold hands when we're out in public."

"To keep up appearances."

Noah took my hand in his and intertwined his fingers with mine. "Exactly, no ulterior motives."

The elevator dinged and we got off, still holding hands. I couldn't help but smile. Noah's hand fit mine perfectly.

"This is nice," I said. "It's been a long time since I met someone who wants to help me and take care of me like this."

"What about your ex? He must've loved you at one point."

"Maybe. I don't know what to believe anymore. That's the thing, you know. As soon as you find out that someone you trusted was lying to you, you start wondering if the entire relationship was a lie."

"Yeah, there's no clear line to tell you which *I love you* was heartfelt and which was just a façade to cover up the betrayal."

We stopped at the Parnassus bar and grabbed an empty table. It was the perfect setting to try to get Noah talking about his past.

"What happened to you exactly? Robert said something about you having been engaged as well?"

A pained look crossed Noah's face, but only briefly. His eyes grew darker and he took a deep breath, then answered my question. "We had been together for only two years when we got engaged. Kate's enthusiasm swept me off my feet right from the get-go. I thought we shared a special bond and that we would have a lifetime full of crazy adventures together. In hindsight, I should've known we weren't compatible. Yes, she loved trying out new things, but she never pushed through. As soon as something else caught her attention, she went for it and forgot all about her previous passions. First she wanted to learn mixology, then it was crochet, then party planning, then baking, and after her short obsession with decorating cookies, she saw the next big shiny thing. Another guy."

"That must've hurt."

"It did, but not necessarily because I'd lost her. I was angry at myself for sticking with a relationship that didn't work. The last couple of months as a couple, we hardly spent any time together. She didn't want to leave the city and I couldn't say goodbye to the peace and calm of my island. She never wanted to meet up with my friends, but expected me to attend every party she was invited to. We were so out of balance, a kid could've seen something didn't add up. I should've let her go long before she cheated on me, but I was afraid."

"Of hurting her?"

"Yes, and of ending up alone. Of starting all over again with someone else. How pathetic, right?"

I put my hand on his and gave it a little squeeze. "It's not pathetic at all, it's human. Starting over can be scary."

Noah tilted his head. "Are you scared?"

"A bit, yes. I'll have to adjust to living on my own again and I don't have the faintest clue about when and where I'll meet someone new. And how to trust them. I think that's the thing that angers me the most. Kyle took that innocent trust from me and I resent him for that."

"The way I see it, you have two choices. Be willing to open your heart again, with the possibility of getting burned, or let your fear stop you from ever finding love again."

A waiter placed our drinks together with a bowl of nacho chips and guacamole on our table, giving me enough time to collect my thoughts. Maybe Noah was right. If I held on to my fear of getting hurt, I would never be able to open up my heart for another man.

"Anger and fear are dangerous. They can consume us if we're

not careful," Noah said, scooping up some guacamole with a chip. "Also, I think that's your phone."

He motioned to my buzzing phone. I picked it up and looked at the screen.

"It's Kyle."

"Maybe you should answer it," Noah said with an encouraging smile.

With my heart nearly beating out of my chest, I pushed the button to accept the call and braced myself for what was coming.

CHAPTER SEVEN

"*H*olly?" Kyle's familiar voice gave me all the feels.

"Hey, Kyle."

"I'm so happy you finally decided to pick up. I've been trying to call you for ages."

"There's hardly any reception at sea," I said.

"At sea?"

"I'm on a cruise. We'll be docking in Grand Cayman tomorrow."

"Sorry, I misunderstood. I thought you said you were on a cruise."

I rolled my eyes, even though he couldn't see how annoyed I was. "Ha-ha, that's funny, Kyle."

"It's just that a cruise is so... not you."

"Well, I guess that proves you don't know me at all. What is it you're calling for?"

I heard him shove some things around, then close a door. "Your stuff. I wanted to agree on a date for you to pick it all up. I know it's not easy, but having your stuff around takes up space and it's kind of inconvenient for Liane."

I closed my eyes and tried to breathe away my anger, but it didn't help.

"Are you still there?" Kyle asked.

"Inconvenient?"

He sighed. "I know it's a rather shitty situation, but can't we be grown-ups about this? Let's not have another fight. Please."

"I'll pick up my stuff when I get back."

"Thank you, Holly. I do hope we can still be friends once the dust settles."

Now, the anger that had come bubbling to the surface spilled over.

"Friends?" My voice came out so loud that several people turned their heads to look at the screaming girl.

Noah looked at me with concern as well. I threw him a smile to reassure him that he didn't have to worry about me. I pushed my chair back and left the Parnassus bar to find a less crowded place on the deck.

"We can never be friends again, not after how you treated me."

"I know I should've told you instead of—"

"Of letting me walk in on you two? In our bed, for crying out loud. It doesn't get any more cliché than that. A real man wouldn't do that to his fiancée."

"What do you want me to say, Holly? I can't help feeling the way I feel."

I balled my hand into a fist and landed it on the railing with a loud thud. "Not once have you told me you're sorry about throwing me out of our apartment. Like I was some old broken toy you didn't want around anymore."

"It wasn't like that. Liane and I have more in common. We're more compatible. She's so funny and pretty."

I scoffed. "Did you just call me ugly?"

"No. I'm just saying that I'm only human and... Liane's a model. I'm sure you can understand what that's like for a guy."

A shrill laugh escaped my mouth. What had I ever seen in that moron? Not only did he have no respect for my feelings or our past together, but he was basically telling me that I wasn't good-looking enough to appeal to his manhood. The tears started streaming down my face, both from sadness and anger.

As I looked up, I saw Noah standing a couple of feet away. The look on his face told me he'd been there long enough to know the conversation was getting out of hand. He walked closer, gently took the phone out of my hand and held it to his ear.

"Hey man, Holly will pick up her stuff once she gets back. I suggest you leave her alone and let her enjoy her vacation."

He was silent for a moment and then continued. "Me? I'm her boyfriend and this is me warning you. Stay the hell away from her. I'm serious."

Noah shook his head and sighed while listening to Kyle's reply. "Yeah, I thought so. Now back off and leave her alone. Oh, and there's one other thing you need to hear loud and clear. One day you'll realize what an amazing girl you let slip between your fingers, but all of your excuses will be too late."

Noah ended the call and handed my phone back. I shoved it in my back pocket with trembling fingers.

"He basically told me I'm stupid and ugly," I said, still sobbing.

Noah stepped closer and cupped my chin with his hands, his eyes fixed on my face. "The guy is a moron. You're the most beautiful girl I've ever seen."

"I don't believe that, but thank you."

He let his index finger trail over my face, all the way from my nose to my lips. The hair on my arms shot straight up and I swallowed away my tears.

"I wouldn't lie to you, Holly. You're pure and real and your soul shines so bright that people love being around you. Don't you ever let anyone tell you differently, especially not someone like Kyle."

All I could do was nod, as I was lost for words. Noah thought I was beautiful? And that my soul shone bright? No man had ever told me something like that. It was almost as if his words shifted something inside of me. As if his words made my fear and anger step down. And I loved how he made me feel more whole again, even though I still had a long road to go.

"Thank you." I whispered the words against Noah's chest and in that moment, the entire world disappeared. All that was left was the cool ocean breeze, Noah's finger still on my lips and his mouth so close I could kiss it if I wanted to.

"Are you up for finishing the food and drinks we ordered or do you want to go back to your cabin?" Noah asked, breaking the spell he had me under.

I stepped out of his embrace and smiled. "Let's eat. It would be a shame to waste a good dip like that."

"That's the spirit," Noah said and we walked back to our table.

"I wanted to shoot some footage for my vlog later on. Maybe we could head to the casino after?"

"Sure."

The more we talked and laughed, the more my anger faded into the background. By the time we set foot in the casino, Kyle's call was nothing more than a distant memory.

We checked out the roulette table. The croupier, who was called Patrick according to his name tag, asked us about our bet and we told him we were going for the ball landing on one of the red squares.

Patrick spun the wheel and the ball started making its rounds, until it finally came to a standstill on a red square.

"We won. We actually won." I jumped up and down and high-fived Noah. "Shall we go again?"

"Or, we can cash our winnings and treat ourselves to a traditional lunch in Grand Cayman tomorrow?" Noah offered.

"Sounds like the perfect plan."

We spent another hour at the casino, trying our luck at one of the slot machines and filming the tacky décor. At eleven, we took the elevator back to our rooms.

We came to a standstill in front of my door.

"Tonight was great. Thank you, Holly."

I shook my head. "No, thank you. And I'm sorry for dragging you into this fake relationship situation."

"It was me who suggested the whole idea. I'm good with it."

Noah bent forward and planted a kiss on my forehead. "Thanks for making this cruise a lot more interesting than I expected it to be. Sleep well."

"You too," I said and watched him walk away.

When he got to the end of the corridor, he turned around again and smiled at me before disappearing around the corner.

I shut my door behind me and let out a breath I didn't even realize I'd been holding. So many thoughts and feelings swirled around inside of me. I'd gone from going on an excursion to ending the day with a fake boyfriend.

As I brushed my teeth, I couldn't stop thinking about Noah. He gave me chills whenever he shot me one of those sparkling smiles, but I had to draw a line for myself. First of all, despite what Georgia might think, he was not into me. Not in a romantic way. And second of all, we would never work outside of this cruise ship. Noah wanted completely different things from life. No matter how amazing he was, I needed to protect myself from falling for him. If I did, there would only be heartbreak and sorrow waiting for me. Still, it didn't hurt to enjoy his company and hugs while it lasted.

Right before I hopped into bed, I scheduled a post for my channel and checked my emails. There was one from Kyle. He didn't know when to call it quits, did he?

Hey Holly,

I just wanted to say: you have no reason to be mad at me since you have clearly moved on yourself. Or is that guy not your real boyfriend?

Anyway, have fun on your cruise and let me know the exact date when you'll be picking up your stuff. Please don't bring your new conquest. That might make it awkward for everyone involved and I don't want that.

Kyle

I shook my head. What had I ever seen in Kyle? He was a jerk. Maybe I should've been happy he cheated on me and removed himself from my life.

I hopped into bed and as I drifted off to sleep, a soft knock woke me back up. It was almost midnight. Who would show up at my door at this late hour? What if it was Logan, who had lost it and wanted to kill me? It was ridiculous, but my imagination went into overdrive.

I lay still and hoped whoever it was would go away, but another knock followed soon enough.

"Holly, it's me. Are you awake?"

I immediately recognized Noah's voice and let out a relieved sigh before opening the door.

"What's up?" I asked, trying not to look straight at him.

He was wearing nothing but a pair of black boxer shorts and his hair was tousled up in the sexiest way possible. In his left hand he was holding a toiletry bag, his toothbrush sticking out at the top.

"I hope I didn't wake you up?"

"I wasn't asleep yet. You were by the looks of it though," I said, which prompted Noah to run a hand through his unruly hair.

"I fled the room, I hope you don't mind."

I stepped aside so he could come in. "What happened?"

He put his toiletry bag down on my desk and grabbed a chair. "Trina is spending the night with Dad. She claimed she saw a ferret in her cabin and doesn't want to set foot in her room anymore."

"A ferret?"

Noah nodded. "At first I thought she was talking about a lion or a hyena. That's how hysterical she was. Anyway, we only have one bed in our cabin and Trina has claimed it. When I protested about not wanting to sleep on the floor, she looked at me like I was crazy and asked me why I didn't want to spend the night at my girlfriend's cabin, so ta-da, here I am."

"I guess this is your lucky night then, because your fake girlfriend has a pull-out sofa."

"Ah, the benefits of having a fake girlfriend with a deluxe room," Noah said with a smile.

"You won't believe the email I got," I said, opening my laptop so he could read the email Kyle had sent me after our phone call.

Noah turned his chair toward the screen, giving me a panoramic view of his muscled back. My heart reacted in all kinds of funny ways, but I pushed the feelings down. We were friends, nothing more.

"There's one thing I can't understand," Noah said, closing the email. "How on earth did a girl like you end up with a creep like that?"

"I've asked myself that question a lot as well these last couple of days."

Noah got up and starting pulling the sofa bed out. "Tomorrow we're going to take some pictures together that will erase every shred of doubt he has about us being a real couple. I know we're only pretending, but I want him to believe we aren't and get that smug smile off his face."

"That smug smile?"

Noah grinned. "That's just how I imagine him typing that email. How do you feel about tomorrow anyway?"

"Good, I guess? Why?" I asked, handing him a pillow and blanket.

"Because we're going stingray swimming, remember?"

I had completely forgotten about the silly promise I'd made that first day, but I couldn't let him down. Not after everything he was doing to help me.

"Don't worry, I'm ready for it," I said, even though I was scared to death to jump into the water with those creatures. At least I'd have Noah there to protect me.

Noah turned off the light and we both crawled under the covers.

"Good night, Holly. Sleep tight."

"Good night," I answered.

Even though I was exhausted, I couldn't fall asleep knowing that Noah was only a couple of feet away from me. I couldn't get the image of him in his underwear out of my head.

I turned to my side. I watched him sleep until my eyes got heavy, and fell asleep to the sound of his breathing.

CHAPTER EIGHT

DAY FOUR: GRAND CAYMAN

I woke up to the gurgling sounds of the coffee machine and for one split second, I was confused about how that was even possible. But when I saw Noah fiddling with cups and milk, it all came back to me. I'd spent the night with him. Well, not in *that* way of course, but he had slept in my room.

Noah had put on my robe and was humming a song, making some dance moves while pouring coffee into two cups.

"You sure are chipper in the morning," I said, rubbing the sleep from my eyes and stretching my arms up high.

"The early bird catches the worm, or in this case, fresh coffee."

He sat himself down on the bed and handed me a mug. "Careful though, it's still hot."

"I could definitely get used to this," I said and cupped the coffee with both hands. "What time is it?"

"Kind of late. The boat has docked already, but you were sleeping so soundly, I didn't want to wake you. The others have already left for Grand Cayman."

"You didn't have to wait for me. I mean, I appreciate it and everything, but I don't want to mess with your plans."

Noah gave me a gentle push. "And not go stingray swimming with you? Nice try."

"Do I at least have time for a quick shower before we leave?"

"Of course, we're on vacation. There's no need to rush."

"Great. I'll meet you at the elevator in twenty," I said.

After a refreshing shower, I put on my bikini, a pair of jean shorts and a loose-fitting shirt. I then shoved my camera, selfie stick, a bottle of water and a towel into my beach bag.

"Let's go meet the stingrays," I said to myself and made my way to the elevator.

Since I was five minutes early, I roamed the hallway to shoot some video material. With one vlog per week, I had to create a lot of content to meet my deadlines. My goal was to make two vlogs about my cruise experience, and the first one was scheduled for next week already.

If I got to one million subscribers by the end of the month, I wouldn't have to go back to working late shifts at the local amusement park over the summer, something I often did when money was tight. I didn't hate it or anything, but it wasn't my true calling.

With Big Bear Co.'s sponsorship deal, I'd finally be able to pay myself a decent income, travel more and start working on another dream of mine: creating a travel book for female solo travelers.

As I was nearing the end of the long corridor, I spotted Logan heading my way. I wanted to turn around and pretend I hadn't seen him, but it was too late. He was already waving at me.

"Hey, Holly," he said.

"Good morning."

He shoved his hands in the pockets of his white Bermuda shorts.

"What do you have planned today?" I asked, trying to fill the silence.

He shrugged. "I don't know. Maybe go to the beach or stay on board. I might check out the activities the Sassy Singles group have planned. You?"

"We're going stingray swimming," I said.

"Oh. Well, that sounds like a lot of fun," he said, the sadness thick in his voice.

Logan still gave me some creepy vibes, but deep down I knew he was harmless. And all alone.

"I guess you could join us if there are any free spots left," I said.

"Us as in you and Noah?" He pronounced the name as if Noah were a serial killer.

I nodded. "I think Georgia and Trina are going as well. Noah said they're already at the beach."

A hand slipped around my waist and I inhaled Noah's familiar scent of honey and sandalwood. "Are you talking about me?"

"I was telling Logan we're going stingray swimming. He might join us."

Noah threw me a concerned look.

"He didn't have any plans yet, so I invited him," I said.

"Let's go then, shall we? The stingray boat leaves in thirty minutes," Noah said.

After a small bus ride, we met Georgia and Trina at the dock where the boat to the stingray sandbar was waiting.

"Good morning, lovebirds. You two sure took your time to get here," Georgia said and winked at us.

"Long night, huh?" Trina said.

"You bet. We hardly got any sleep," Noah said and planted a kiss on the top of my head. He was having the best time misleading everyone.

"Where are the others?" I asked. Trina pulled out her phone, showing us a picture of Robert and George. They were sitting in beach chairs, each wearing a big hat to guard them from the sun.

"They're soaking up the sun already. And Mindy went for a stroll around town."

"Doesn't your dad get tired of wearing that life vest all the time?" I asked Noah. "It looks uncomfortable and way too hot."

"He does take it off at night," Trina said with a smile that said more than words ever could.

Noah rolled his eyes. "That's intel you can keep behind closed doors."

Trina waved his remark away with her hand and continued. "There's no shame in knowing your dad is still doing great in the bedroom department. I was pleasantly surprised by his skills and tenderness."

Georgia chuckled and patted Trina on the arm. "The joys of an older man, am I right?"

"Totally. I never knew it could be like that."

Noah put his hands on his chest and made a gagging sound.

"Fine, no more bedroom talk," Trina said with a roll of her eyes. "Let's go, shall we?"

We all got on the catamaran and I immediately went for one of the spots at the front of the boat. There were two nets on either side of the mast, serving as a laid-back seating area.

I let my feet dangle off the side of the catamaran and shoved my shirt into my bag. The sun was already burning bright, even though it wasn't noon yet.

"Do you need some help?" Noah asked, holding up a bottle of sunscreen.

"Definitely."

He positioned himself behind me and sprayed some sunscreen on my back. He made firm circles with his hands, spreading the liquid everywhere. A moan escaped my mouth.

"I'll have what she's having," Georgia called out from the middle of the boat.

"We've got to make this boyfriend-girlfriend thing believable, hence the moan," I said with a whisper. "Your astounding massage skills have got nothing to do with it."

"Of course. That wasn't a bedroom noise at all."

I slapped him on the arm, not able to contain my smile. "Stop it, you don't know what I sound like in the bedroom."

"You did snore last night, I can tell you that much."

Noah winked at me and my stomach got all fuzzy. The more hours and days passed, the more I longed for his touch, even though it was useless. This was a vacation from real life and we didn't have a shot once we set foot in Miami again. We lived completely different lives. He on an island, me traveling all the time.

The boat started moving and Tuda, our guide, gave a safety demonstration. He showed us how to use a life vest, then talked about what to do in case of an emergency. It was the perfect segue to focus on something other than Noah's abs and bright green eyes.

"Sit back and relax, everyone. First stop, the Stingray City Sandbar," Tuda announced, putting the life vests away again.

The catamaran sailed away, blue water stretching out in front of us. Trina was lying on a beach towel, soaking up the sun, and Logan had found a spot at the other side of the boat.

"Are you afraid he's posting bikini pics of you again?" Noah asked, following my gaze to where Logan was twiddling on his phone.

"Nah. I think he's just lonely," I said.

Noah smiled. "Is that why you invited him?"

"Kind of. I feel sorry for him. Is that bad? I mean, I wouldn't want someone taking pity on me. Like, imagine if you were doing all of this because you felt sorry for me. I'd be mortified."

"I do sympathize with your situation, but I don't pity you. I love spending time with you, regardless of what label we've given this relationship." He briefly touched my arm, and it gave me goosebumps all over.

"Isn't this cozy? You two are such an adorable couple," Georgia said, clapping her hands as if she was witnessing two baby ducks hitting the water for the first time.

"Aw, thank you, Georgia," I said.

"Do you mind if I borrow your man for a second? I need someone to put sunscreen on my back. George would kill me if he found out I was out in the sun unprotected for longer than a millisecond."

I let out a laugh. "Go ahead, he's a pro when it comes to sunscreen."

"Take a seat," Noah said, reaching for the bottle of SPF50 in his backpack.

While Noah worked his magic on Georgia, I took my camera and walked around to film the sparkling water surrounding the boat. The view was perfect and in such stark contrast to my life back at home.

I sucked in my bottom lip. Home. I didn't even know where to call home now that Kyle had kicked me out of our apartment. I had spent the last couple of weeks at a friend's place, but she had a life of her own. I needed to find a more permanent solution soon.

"A penny for your thoughts." Trina startled me and I almost dropped my camera.

"I was just shooting some clips for my channel, nothing special."

She looked back to where Noah was sitting and gave my shoulder a push with hers. "So, are we lucky to have found these men or what? We might even become family if you decide to marry Noah and I marry Robert."

"Yeah, who knows? But it's only been a couple of days. Marriage has not crossed my mind yet."

Trina looked out at the ocean and sighed. "It has crossed mine. I know Robert's more than double my age, but it's like he's my missing puzzle piece, you know?"

I nodded, even though I didn't know. A pang of jealousy went through me. She had found love and I had found, well, the fake kind of love. I guessed it was better than nothing at all.

"And if you marry Noah, you can live on his island. How cool would that be?"

"It's not technically his island, but yeah, that would be heaven."

Trina arched her eyebrow. "Huh. I swear Robert said Noah owns an island."

"I don't really know the specifics, to be honest."

She wiggled her eyebrows. "I get it. You two are too busy... you know."

I laughed her comment away and gazed into the distance. I needed a moment to process what she had just told me. How on earth had Noah been able to afford a private island? Or had Trina misunderstood and she was talking about the island Noah took care of? She could've easily gotten her wires crossed.

"Looks like we're here," Trina said, pointing to a spot nearby where several other catamarans and small boats had gathered.

A group of people were standing in the ocean, the water reaching up to their waists.

"Welcome to Stingray City Sandbar," Tuda said and fiddled with some ropes.

Noah walked over to me and put his arm around my shoulders. "Looks like it's time to go and play with the stingrays."

"You're enjoying this way too much," I said.

"I am, *honey*," he said, giving me a look that made it clear he wasn't talking about the stingrays at all.

CHAPTER NINE

"I'm going in." Georgia hit the water first, squealing with delight. For a woman in her sixties, she sure wasn't afraid of much. Not that this situation was anything to get the adrenaline going, but I didn't like big fish.

I lowered myself into the water and my body tensed. One of the girls who was already in the water fed a small fish to one of the stingrays. She screamed as soon as the creature grabbed the fish from her hands.

"I'm not sure about this," I said, clasping Noah's arm.

"Don't worry, nothing bad can happen. Although this entire thing looks nothing like I'd imagined it."

"What? Water and weirdly-shaped fish that are as thin as pancakes?"

He chuckled. "No. There's so many people. Not to mention the *let's take a picture with a stingray to put on social media* thing. It's tacky."

"I agree," I said. "I don't like these overly touristy places either, but you were the one who dragged us down here, so you might as well enjoy it. Or we can stay on the boat."

"No way. We're going in."

We waded through the water and joined the rest of our group. Tuda got a hold of one of the stingrays, and let the animal touch his face. Why on earth someone would want to do that was beyond me, but almost immediately two men stated they wanted to kiss a stingray as well.

We waited for them to get a picture, and I let my gaze wander in an attempt to let my fear ebb away.

"Is that Logan without his socks on? Have you ever seen such a sight?" A laugh played on Noah's lips.

"Shut up, he might hear you."

"And realize wearing socks in sandals all day is a weird fashion choice?"

I shrugged. "I'd hardly call it a fashion choice, but whatever it is, it's not nice to make fun of people. Also, what are you doing with your foot?"

Noah looked down into the water. "My foot is doing nothing, but there is a stingray at your legs."

"What?" I shrieked so loud that everyone stopped talking.

"It's okay, these stingrays are harmless," Tuda said. "Why don't you come on up and take a picture with them?"

He was still holding the kissing stingray with his hands. All I wanted to do was get back to the boat and out of the water, but I had a promise to keep. Besides, I didn't want Noah to think I was one of those girls who was afraid of everything. I would suck it up and go for it.

Noah and I waded over to Tuda, and we scooted together for a picture.

"How about a little kiss?" Tuda asked.

"I'm not kissing that thing," I said.

"No, I mean you and your man. Show him some love for the picture."

My face flushed. I looked at Noah. The others let out a cheer, and I could feel their eyes on us, waiting for Noah and I to make our move.

"Young love, so beautiful," I heard Georgia say with a sigh.

"I'm game if you are?" Noah asked. I nodded, ready to feel those lips on mine, even though it wouldn't be a real kiss.

He leaned in. I could feel his warm breath on my cheeks. A couple of inches closer and his lips would touch mine. He looked me in the eye with a smile that made my body turn into jelly, then cupped my neck with his hand. With his other hand, he swept a string of hair to the side.

Gosh, he sure was taking his sweet time for this kiss. I pulled my eyes away from his and looked down at his mouth, until all I felt were our lips touching for the first time. Noah tasted like the sweetest and ripest fruit on a hot summer day, making me crave more. He held the kiss for at least five seconds before gently pulling away again.

Wow. My mind had turned into mush and I couldn't think straight anymore. I didn't even care about the stingrays that were touching my legs.

If what I had just experienced was a fake kiss, how would a real one with him feel? I couldn't imagine it being any better than what I'd just experienced.

Tuda handed Noah's camera back and we waded through the water. I climbed the ladder to the boat and sat myself down on a towel, dazed and confused.

"I hope that wasn't too much," Noah said, throwing me a worried look.

I shook my head and squeezed his hand. "It wasn't. It was kind of perfect, to be honest."

"I thought so, too." He ran his thumb over my hand and I had to do everything I could not to kiss him again. Technically, no one would think it was weird. We were supposed to be a couple after all. But my heart told me not to cross that line. I'd be lost and the door to heartbreak would be right open again.

Three hours later, we joined Robert and George at Seven Mile Beach. Robert still wouldn't part ways with his beloved life vest, even though he didn't even set foot in the shallow water of the ocean stretching out in front of us.

The beach was packed with people, from couples to groups of friends to families with young kids. All along the beach were rows and rows of fancy hotels and restaurants. It looked like heaven, apart from the crowds. If I had been on one of my solo travels, I'd have gone off and found a more secluded area.

"Your son and Holly shared the most romantic moment at the Stingray City Sandbar," Trina said while holding Robert's hand. "It was magical."

Robert smiled at Noah "And to think just months ago you said you didn't want to get involved with anyone ever again. Guess you never know what life will throw your way, do you?"

Noah clearly didn't feel like smiling back. His eyes clouded and he sprang to his feet, grabbing a bottle of water out of his backpack.

"I'm going for a short walk," he announced.

"Mind if I join you?" I asked. "I want to film before I soak up some sun."

He threw me an apologetic look and touched my arm. "I'd love to stroll the beach with you, but I need some time alone. We'll catch up after?"

"Sure," I said and gave him my biggest smile. Inside I was shaking though. Why didn't he want me to come with him?

The atmosphere tensed as I watched Noah walk away, his bare feet wading through the shallows.

"I'll go with you," Logan offered. "I don't like sitting on the beach and doing nothing."

Great, just what I needed, a couple of hours to talk about Star Trek and listen to math jokes, when all I could think about was Noah not wanting me around all of a sudden.

"I feel like us girls need some time to ourselves, am I right? No offense, Logan," Georgia said, threading her arm through mine.

Trina looked up at us. "Do you mind if I stay here though? I kind of missed Robert this morning and I don't want to leave him alone again."

"I guess it's just the two of us then."

Georgia started walking and I followed suit.

"I'm sorry to blow Logan off like that, but I sensed you needed someone to talk to who understands what it's like to be a woman."

"Thank you. I appreciate it."

We walked in silence for five minutes and I tried to collect my thoughts. Noah and I had shared such a great morning, with that astonishing kiss as the cherry on top. And now he wanted to be alone. Maybe he was having second thoughts about us faking a relationship?

The worst thing was that he was probably right. It was not his job to keep me safe. It was my own responsibility to be firm and set my boundaries. I couldn't expect him to spend every minute of his well-deserved holiday with me.

"Are you alright, sweetie? You didn't expect Noah to go off without you, did you now?" Georgia asked, eyeing me with concern.

"He has a right to live his own life."

We stopped at a gelato stand and ordered ourselves an ice cream cone before continuing our walk.

"You know you can talk to me, right? I might be old, but I do know a thing or two about love."

I smiled and my heart broke. She was being so sweet and kind to me that lying to her didn't seem right.

"If I tell you something, will you promise to keep it to yourself?" I asked.

"Of course."

I licked my ice cream and sighed. "We made it all up to give Logan a reason not to bother me. We thought it would be fun. That's a bad thing to do, I know."

"I figured something didn't add up."

"You did?"

"Like I said, I know a thing or two about love. You want to hear my take on this whole situation?"

I nodded. "Please."

"The reasons for faking your relationship don't matter. What does matter is the fact that Noah is madly in love with you, whether you believe it or not."

I threw my head back and laughed so hard that I almost choked on my ice cream. "Georgia, didn't you hear what I just said? It's all fake. We agreed to pretend to be boyfriend and girlfriend. There's no love between us. Not the real kind anyway."

She put a hand on her hip, giving me a look. "He's madly in love with you, sweetie, believe me. I had my doubts at first, but this morning changed everything."

"This morning?"

Georgia smiled. "At the Stingray City Sandbar. You can't fake a kiss like that."

"I don't know."

"You'll come to see the truth eventually. Just don't wait too long or it might be too late."

"If that's true, then why did he ditch me just now? It doesn't make any sense."

Georgia shrugged. "He's still a guy. Who knows what goes on in their heads?"

I laughed. "I wish I knew. It would make life a lot easier."

"Why don't you ask him?"

I followed Georgia's gaze and spotted Noah in the distance. He was sitting cross-legged, scooping up sand with his hands and letting it filter through his fingers.

I took a deep breath.

"I don't know. I think it would be better if he came to me. Not that I don't want to talk, but he did want to be alone and I'm guessing there's a good reason for that. I'm sure that he'll tell me once he's ready."

"Fair enough," Georgia said.

I was relieved that she didn't press the issue. Deep down, I wanted nothing more than to run over to him and ask him what was wrong, but it was no use. And what would I do once I had his answer? What if he told me it was something I did or said that made him back away? I'd rather not know at all.

There was only one thing I could do, and that was shove any budding feelings I had for him into a box and keep them locked in there.

CHAPTER TEN

DAY FIVE: COZUMEL

I woke up at the crack of dawn, after a restless night of tossing and turning. Since it was only seven a.m., I skipped breakfast and got ready to shoot some footage of the still-empty ship.

Noah had stayed in his room after we returned from Grand Cayman and all I'd heard from him since was a short message asking me to meet him at nine for our last excursion of the week.

I roamed around the ship, enjoying the fact that almost everyone was still asleep. It was nice not to be surrounded by people for once and get some breathing room so I could be alone with my thoughts.

With only two days left, the end of the cruise was creeping closer and I didn't know if that was a good thing or not. On the one hand it was time for me to get my ducks in a row, move my stuff out of Kyle's place and make a fresh start. But on the other hand it also meant saying goodbye to Noah. Not once had we talked about a future outside of the ship, and why would we? We were only pretending, so there would be no reason for us to keep seeing each other as soon as we docked in Miami. Even if there was something going on between us, it could never work. I spent my days traveling, surrounded by people, always looking for a new adventure, whereas Noah spent his time on a deserted island. Our worlds were too far apart.

As I walked past the spa, I bumped into a group of girls standing in front of a closed door.

"Are you here for the pole class as well?" a girl with a pixie cut asked me.

"No, I'm just exploring this deck. I haven't had the chance to come up here yet."

"Why don't you join us? Janey, the teacher, is really good and it's a lot of fun. Class starts at eight. And I swear these classes make you feel sexy and empowered like never before."

I checked the time on my phone. I could squeeze in a pole class before meeting Noah.

"Sure, why not?"

"You're going to love it," one of the other girls stated.

While we waited for the class to start, the girls filled me in on what they'd already learnt that week. Apparently they had been there every morning, which made me curious to know what was so great about these classes that they kept coming back for more.

At eight on the dot, the doors to the dance studio opened and we all got into position.

"Good morning, everyone," the instructor said. "My name is Janey."

She talked a bit about her background, then told us to grab a pair of shoes from a basket in the back of the room.

Janey jumped straight into a warm-up session with squats, stretches, leg lifts and sit-ups. By the time the warm-up was done, I was sweating all over. I didn't have to think about Noah or Kyle or work. All I had to do was focus on my body, a liberating experience.

"Now we're going to try out some of the basics," Janey said. "Remember: don't be shy."

She had us walking around the pole, then rocking our hips back and forth. At first I felt ridiculous making those movements, but Janey's encouraging words helped me relax with every move.

Letting go and leaving all of my worries behind lifted my spirits. I loved moving around the pole and wondered if that was how a goddess felt: free, sassy and proud of her body. It was exhilarating.

By the end of the class I was panting and sweating, but with a big smile on my face.

"This was exactly what I needed," I told the girl with the pixie cut. "Thank you for inviting me."

"It feels good, right? Why don't you come back tomorrow? We'll all be here as well."

I nodded. "I might do that, thank you."

It was already close to nine, so I fired off a message to Noah to tell him I was running a little late. Since I had no time for a shower, I went into the bathroom next to the spa and freshened up at the sink. After a spritz of deodorant and a fresh layer of mascara, I was ready to go meet Noah and visit Cozumel.

Noah was waiting for me next to the elevators. His face lit up when our eyes met.

"Good morning," I said, feeling like I could handle anything he would throw at me after that pole class.

"Did you sleep well?" he asked.

"Not really, but I'm completely energized again. I went to a pole class. It was absolutely amazing."

He grinned. "I wish I had been there to see you twirl around a pole."

"You could join me tomorrow. There's classes every day."

"I don't think pole dancing is my thing, but thanks."

As we waited to get off the boat, Noah turned to me and grabbed my hand. "I'm sorry about ditching you like that yesterday."

"It's okay," I said.

"I needed some time alone to think some things through, but I assure you that it's got nothing to do with you. I want you to know that."

"Really, it's okay. We're friends and friends have to give each other some breathing room from time to time."

"Yeah, friends."

"What are the others up to today?" I asked, trying to steer the conversation in another direction.

"Honestly, I don't have a clue. Today is about you and me."

"It is?"

He shrugged. "It's the last stop of the cruise before we return to Miami. I want to spend it with my girlfriend."

I craned my neck and looked around. "Oh yeah? I don't see her anywhere. Are you sure she's coming?"

Noah laughed and pulled me closer. "Just because the others aren't around doesn't mean we can't keep up appearances."

Now he wanted to keep up appearances? Men could be so confusing. Leaving one minute, wanting to be near you the next. I would never get them, but then again, what man understood what made women tick? Hell, *I* didn't even know what made women tick.

Disembarking the ship went smoothly and minutes later we set foot on Mexican soil. I got my camera out and was met by a look from Noah that spoke volumes.

"Do you always have to be filming? No offense, but it's like you're glued to the thing twenty-four seven."

"It's all part of the job. Besides, I don't get my camera out that much," I countered.

"You do know addicts have a hard time admitting they have an addiction, right?"

I slapped him with my bag. "Aren't you full of humor today."

He grinned at me and my heart skipped a beat.

"As long as you don't show my face in your vlogs too often."

"You don't like to be in the spotlight, do you?"

"Not really."

Noah stopped at a wooden sign that had a map of the island plastered on it. "Where do you want to go today?"

It was as if those words had magic to them, because as soon as they left Noah's mouth we found ourselves surrounded by eager sales people, all wanting to sell their services to us.

I knew from experience that we shouldn't settle for the first offer that came our way, so we took our sweet time to find something we would both enjoy.

We decided on a salsa tour at Playa Mia Grand Beach that focused on all kinds of salsa: both the dip and the dance.

"I'm going to grab a breakfast burrito before we leave though. I didn't have breakfast yet," I said and stopped at a street cart. "Do you want one?"

Noah shook his head. "I'm still full from breakfast."

After I paid for my burrito, we walked to the beach to find the building where the salsa workshop was going to go down.

"So, what are your plans after we return to Miami?" I asked, taking a bite of my burrito.

"Head back home. One week is long enough to be away from the island. There's work to be done."

"Like swing in your hammock?"

Noah laughed. "No, like repair the fishing nets, check the motor boats for damage, mow the lawn."

"You have a lawn to mow on a private island?"

"Well, yeah. It's a deserted island, but not like the one

Robinson Crusoe lived on. I don't go out hunting and gathering supplies."

"Trina said you own the island?" I needed to know if it was true.

He shot me a sideways glance and shrugged. "Maybe. I haven't decided yet."

Now it was my turn to laugh. "You don't know whether or not you own a private island?"

"Someone gave it to me, but I don't know if I want to accept the gift."

This was unbelievable. If someone gave me a private million-dollar island, I wouldn't hesitate to call it mine.

"Why not? That's crazy. For one, your net worth would... I don't know, go through the roof. And you'd never have to worry about mortgage payments or work and you'd be able to live in paradise. What doubts could you possibly have?"

We stopped in front of our destination and I looked up at Noah, who was towering over me as usual. Only this time he looked so sad that I regretted bringing the whole island thing up.

"I'm sorry, it's none of my business and you don't have to answer me," I said. "I wouldn't tell a stranger about my personal dealings either."

Noah grabbed my hand. "You're not a stranger, Holly. It's complicated, that's all. The island belonged to Kate's father and he gave it to me after we split. I think he did it because he felt bad about what happened. It's his way to apologize for his daughter's behavior, even though it's not his fault. I'm supposed to sign the final documents next week and then the island is mine. But I don't know if I want to. I know Kate and I have no future together, but we share a history and, well... I'm still finding it difficult to come to terms with all these changes."

"I get that. Love can be messy. But maybe it could be a new start for you. Having an island creates a ton of possibilities."

Noah threw me a thin smile. "Maybe. I've still got time to decide."

"I promise I won't bring it up again. Let's go make some salsa." I hooked my arm through his and together we walked up the steps to our last excursion.

◔

After an hour of mixing, grinding and squeezing, we'd made guacamole, red salsa and pico de gallo together. The dips all tasted delicious and fresh, a big contrast to the premade ones I normally bought at the supermarket.

My stomach was a bit upset though, but I attributed my queasiness to the fact that the bartender kept bringing us tasty margaritas.

"I don't think I need another refill," I told Noah as we finished the last of our salsa with a bowl of corn chips. "I'm not feeling too great."

Concern filled his eyes and he put his palm to my forehead. "You do feel kind of warm. Are you sure it's the alcohol?"

"Definitely. Alcohol in this weather might not have been the best of choices."

"I'll get you a water. You're probably just dehydrated."

My stomach made an ominous gurgling sound and I clutched my belly with both hands while Noah walked away. I should've stuck to nonalcoholic drinks, but the margaritas had looked divine.

Noah put a bottle of water down on the table in front of me. "Here, drink up. Are you sure you'll be able to dance? I heard someone say there's ninety minutes of salsa dancing."

I took a big swig of water and waved away his concern. "I'll be fine, don't worry."

"If you start feeling worse, let me know, okay?"

I nodded. "I will, thanks."

We got called into an adjacent room for the salsa dancing and even though I had initially looked forward to it, I was starting to have second thoughts. The twisting and turning of my stomach worsened and I started to get dizzy. I figured I'd be fine though, if I could just hang on for a couple more hours.

The class started simple enough, with moving our legs back and forth, then sideways. But fifteen minutes in things started to pick up speed, which only made my dizziness worse.

Noah threw me a look, asking me if I was feeling okay. I confirmed I did by sticking both of my thumbs in the air. I didn't want my queasiness to ruin his day.

Half an hour later, I changed my mind. All the moving around had made things worse and I started to realize that this was not just a case of drinking too many margaritas on a hot day. It was something way worse.

"Holly, are you sure you're okay?" Noah asked. "Why don't you sit down?" He'd stopped dancing and was looking at me as if I was about to die.

"I think that's a good idea," I said.

He held out his hand for me, but I missed grabbing it as the entire room started to spin. I could see Noah talking to me, but didn't hear a word he said as everything suddenly went black.

CHAPTER ELEVEN

I opened my eyes and my confused look was met by four people huddled around me. It took me a moment before I remembered where I was and what had happened.

"Good, you're back," Noah said.

"Miss, are you okay?" one of the workshop ladies asked me, a scared look on her face.

"She looks as pale as a sheet," someone else said.

"We should call an ambulance."

All their voices flew around me, but I could only concentrate on one thing: the wave of nausea hitting me like a car crashing into a wall.

"I think I'm going to be sick," I said with a pleading look at Noah. The last thing I wanted to do was throw up in the middle of the dance floor.

Noah quickly helped me get up and offered me his arm for support. It took me a lot of effort to walk even the short distance to the toilet.

"Quick," I said, feeling my stomach clench.

We arrived at the bathroom area just in time for my breakfast burrito to make a reappearance. Gosh, what on earth had caused this? And why did I have to get sick in front of Noah? It was anything but sexy.

Noah grabbed a handful of toilet paper and dabbed my head with it. After throwing them in the bin, he held his hand against my head.

"You're burning up, Holly. I'm taking you back to the ship so you can get medical help right away. Do you think you can walk?"

"I want to stay here," I said.

"On the floor of a bathroom stall?"

I nodded. "It beats walking."

"It's only five minutes to the ship. After the doctor checks you out, you can slip under the covers and rest. Wouldn't you rather be under a duvet in a comfortable room than out here?"

I sighed. "Yes. But I can't get there. And I don't want to get into a car either, because I'll throw up in it."

Tears stung my eyes as another wave of nausea rolled over me.

"Don't worry about any of that. I'll help you. Let me get you a bottle of water and then we'll leave."

As soon as Noah left to buy some water, I hovered above the toilet again. The pain in my stomach was unbearable. If giving birth could be compared to this, I swore I'd never have kids.

When Noah got back, he urged me to drink some water before handing me a plastic bag. "I fixed us a ride and this bag, so you don't have to worry about ruining the car."

"Thank you," I said.

We got into the car and I closed my eyes, trying to breathe the nausea away. My hair stuck to the back of my neck and with every bump in the road that the driver hit, I had to do my best not to use the bag Noah had given me.

I thanked the heavens that we hadn't gone to the ancient city of Tulum like I'd first planned. I didn't know how I would've survived a long bus trip feeling the way I did.

"Is there something I can do?" Noah asked, putting a hand on my damp shirt and creasing his brow in what I could only imagine was pure concern.

"Teleport me to my room?"

"Isn't that some kind of Star Trek trick? If so, I can call Logan and ask him to beam you up."

I smiled weakly at his joke. Not because I didn't think it was funny, but because all of the energy I had was slowly but surely seeping out of me like a deflating balloon.

"These are the longest five minutes of my life," I whispered.

Noah glanced at the road ahead. "We're almost back at the pier."

I closed my eyes again, and a swirl of geometric shapes appeared in front of me. Maybe I wasn't sick after all. Maybe I was losing it for real and going crazy? Or maybe there had been some kind of drug in the salsa we made? But if that were true, then why did Noah seem unharmed?

The thud of a car door slamming startled me.

"We're here," Noah said.

He held out his hand and I gratefully took it. Without him, I wouldn't have known how to stay upright.

I squeezed the plastic bag so tight my hand shook, but all the squeezing in the world couldn't stop me from vomiting again.

"I'm sorry. This must be a horrible sight." I was on the edge of losing my sanity.

"All I care about is getting you on that ship and to a doctor. Stop worrying about anything else," Noah said.

He whipped out a tissue from his pants pocket and wiped my mouth, then handed me the bottle of water again.

"How come you know exactly what I need? I wish I could

keep you," I said, trying to keep my eyes focused on the pier that led toward the ship's entrance.

"Alright, Holly, lean on me and take it slow," Noah said, putting an arm around me for support.

Even though we were only walking across the dock toward the ship, it felt as if I was climbing a mountain. I needed all of my strength and courage to do so. The other people strolling happily around seemed alien to me. How could they be so chipper and carefree? The way they smiled and frisked around was in such strong contrast to my own snail-like movements.

"I feel like a mop cloth being dragged across the floor," I said. "What if I'm going crazy?"

"You're not, you have a fever. It makes you act weird, that's all," Noah said with a reassuring smile.

"What if the ship leaves before I get there?"

Noah stopped and took my hands in his. "The ship won't leave for hours. We're fine. Really, there's no reason to be afraid."

When we finally got back onto the ship, I couldn't wait to crawl under the covers, but Noah insisted we take the elevator to visit the medical facility first.

I slid into one of the plastic chairs in the waiting room. "How long will this take? I can't do this. I need to lie down. I'm sure it's just a harmless tummy bug."

I didn't want to sound like a whiny person, but for some reason I couldn't help myself. This was definitely not the right occasion to practice mind over matter. Matter was taking over big time and I didn't have the energy to fight it.

Five long minutes later, we got called into one of the examination rooms where we were greeted by a doctor.

"Hi, Holly, I'm Dr. Walsh. How can I help you today?"

"I feel bad. Sick. Hot," I said.

Noah smiled at the doctor and gave a more elaborate response, explaining to him what exactly had happened and where we were when I fainted. Dr. Walsh let me lie down on the examination table while he pulled a pair of latex gloves out of a box on his desk.

"When did you start feeling nauseous?"

"About two hours ago," I said.

The doctor touched my abdomen and I cringed. "Does this hurt?"

I nodded. "Like hell."

After some more prodding and questions about what I had eaten and my water intake, and a quick temperature check, Dr. Walsh scribbled some things down on a pad. He folded his hands and looked at me.

"All the symptoms you have point to food poisoning. You'll need to rest, drink lots of fluids and take some medication to keep you from dehydrating. I strongly suggest your boyfriend here keeps a close eye on you. If there are any signs of this getting worse, like a loss of vision, extreme dizziness and the fever not going down, or if your urine is more yellow than usual, you have to call the medical facility asap."

Great. So Noah had to stay with me and check the color of my pee? Not what I had in mind for our second-to-last day on this cruise.

"When in doubt, call. It's better to have a false alarm than one that's way overdue."

"Was it the salsa?" I asked.

"It could've been the breakfast burrito," Noah said. "That's the only thing you ate that I didn't."

If that was true, I never wanted to eat a damn burrito again. He was probably right. Who knew how long that thing had been out there in the sun before I ate it?

"I have to throw up."

Dr. Walsh quickly shoved a metal kidney dish under my mouth.

"I'm sorry," I said after I was finished.

Dr. Walsh threw me a warm smile. "I've seen worse, believe me."

He rummaged through a drawer and handed me a pack of barf bags. "Here, take these to your room. You'll need them."

We thanked him and Noah led me to my room. I got my keycard out of my pocket. After opening the door I stumbled toward the bed while my fake boyfriend closed the curtains.

Noah took my shoes off and tucked me under the covers. I let out a relieved sigh.

"This bed is a little slice of heaven in hell," I said, mumbling the words.

He laughed. "I told you cruise ships were hellish places, didn't I?"

I nodded. He had uttered those words, that first day on the deck. I smiled at the memory, then drifted off to sleep.

I woke up lying in Noah's arms. He kept repeating that it was okay.

"What? What happened? What's okay?"

"You had a bad dream. Screamed something about drowning?"

"We're at sea," I said, feeling my eyes get heavy again. "There's water everywhere."

He dabbed my face with a damp washcloth. "You're okay, go back to sleep. The more rest you get, the faster you'll heal."

"I'm cold. Why is it freezing in here?"

Noah lay back down beside me. "The fever is making you shiver. Just sleep, Holly. It's the best medicine."

A while later, I got jerked out of a bad dream again. I clawed in the bed, trying to find Noah. I pushed myself up on my elbows. He was standing at the foot of the bed.

"Don't leave," I said. "I'll die without you here."

"I was just making some coffee. I'm not going anywhere. And no one's going to die either."

He put his mug down and sat down beside me, a thermometer in his hands. I let him put it in my mouth. Then he held my head up so I could drink, and handed me a fresh pillow as the one I was sleeping on was soaked with feverish sweat.

"Am I dreaming?" I asked, Noah's face hovering above me.

He pulled the covers up to my chin and flattened the edges. "This is all too real unfortunately. You've got food poisoning, remember?"

A vague image of a breakfast burrito, salsa dip and kidney bowls drifted before my eyes. My stomach turned again, but nothing came out.

Noah readjusted my pillow once more and I sighed.

"You're pretty," I said into his beautiful eyes.

He touched my nose with his index finger and opened his mouth as if to speak, but said nothing. Instead, he got up and turned off the coffee maker.

"If it's okay with you, I'm going upstairs for dinner. I won't be long, okay? Oh, and I'll bring you some bread rolls for when you feel better."

"I wish you were my real boyfriend," I said before I once again got sucked under a heavy blanket of sleep.

CHAPTER TWELVE

*W*hen I woke again, it was pitch dark outside. I had no idea what time it was and I felt too weak to get my phone and check.

My hair stuck to my face. My clothes were drenched with sweat. I longed for a shower and handfuls of soap, but I didn't have the strength to get to the bathroom by myself.

"Noah?" My voice sounded dry and harsh.

"Yes, I'm here."

I heard some fumbling near the sofa bed. Noah appeared from under the covers and sat himself down on the edge of the bed, rubbing the sleep from his eyes. His dark hair was completely messed up, and he was wearing nothing but a pair of boxer shorts. He looked irresistible in the moonlight.

"I think I need a shower," I said.

"Good."

"Good? Are you saying I stink?"

He laughed. "No. You wanting to get out of bed to take a shower is a good sign. It means the worst is over. I'll help you."

He walked into the bathroom, flipped on the light and turned the shower on.

I got up, feeling dizzy, but made it to the closet on my own. I longed to get out of those damp clothes and put on a fresh shirt. I grabbed a clean bra, clean briefs and my favorite tank top, plus a comfy pair of shorts, and inched toward the bathroom.

"The temperature should be good. Call me if you need any help," Noah said before closing the door behind him.

The water felt like gold on my skin. With shaky hands, I washed my hair and body. The scent of my body scrub filled the air and I took a deep breath in. It was good to feel alive again, even though I was only at like twenty percent of my full energy level.

After toweling myself dry, I brushed my teeth.

"Can you grab my body lotion?" I asked Noah. "It's in my bag."

"Which one?" he called from the other side of the bathroom door.

"The one I took with me to the salsa workshop. It's a blue one and the body lotion is a little pink tube with golden letters."

I waited for Noah to tell me he'd found it, but there was nothing but silence coming from the room. I put on my underwear and opened the bathroom door. Noah was sitting on the bed with a look that made me positive he'd been attacked by a giant spider. Or maybe that loose ferret was running around in there.

"What's wrong?"

He looked up at me. "I'm so, so sorry, Holly. Everything went so fast and all I could think about was getting help and..."

Dread coursed through me and I almost didn't want to hear what he was going to say next. "And?"

"I forgot to grab your bag when we left the workshop. Was there anything important in it? Please don't tell me there was."

I sat down on the bed and could feel the blood leave my face. This was bad, really bad. This was... a true disaster.

"Why? How? Why?"

"I'm sure if we call the salsa place when we get back to the mainland they will be able to send it to you."

"If no one stole it, you mean. My phone was in there. And my camera. I need that footage for my next video and for that deal with Big Bear Co. Even if whoever found it kept it in a safe place, there's no way I'll be able to get my hands on it again before my next deadline."

Noah put his hand on my leg. "I know, but you can just use your backup files, can't you? Problem solved."

I blinked. "I don't have any backup files."

He arched his brow. "You don't? Everyone knows you need backup files."

His words punched me in the gut. "Are you're trying to say I'm dumb? I've never needed backup files. This has never happened to me."

I didn't mean to yell, but the panic inside of me was taking over. How was I going to fix this? It wasn't like I could shoot some new footage on the ship and be done with it. I needed the entire thing, from beginning to end.

"Calm down, Holly. It's not my fault this happened, you know."

I shook my head, tears rolling down my cheeks. "I thought I could trust you."

Noah held his hands up. "Whoa, trust me? I've been here for more than twelve hours, taking care of you, making sure your condition didn't get worse. I've even pretended to be your boyfriend this past week. And then you accuse me of not being trustworthy? Does that sound fair to you?"

"I meant, trust you to take care of my stuff."

Noah got up, hurt written all over his face. "Well, excuse me for wanting to take care of you instead of your stuff. A bag full of things can be replaced, you know, a person can't."

I shook my head. "I didn't mean it to come out like that. You taking care of me was something I'm truly grateful for. I guess I'm just shook up from losing my footage and vomiting all night long."

"Maybe I should go," he said.

"No, please, don't go," I pleaded and grabbed his hand.

"It's okay. We both know this has to end eventually."

"What do you mean, *this*?"

He motioned from me to himself. "This. Us. Last time I opened up my heart for someone I truly liked, it didn't work out either. I was convinced I made her happy until one day she told me I wasn't the kind of guy she wanted to be with. I tried to be the perfect boyfriend and couldn't. I tried to see past our differences, but it was no use. Why would it be any different this time? I've learned my lesson and I know I'm better off alone."

"No one is better off alone."

"Some people are."

I swallowed hard. "Noah, I'm so sorry about what I said."

He sighed. "It's okay. I would be pretty shaken too if I'd lost something important. But I meant what I said about this not working. I know exactly how this is going to pan out. I'll try to make you happy and sooner or later, I'll screw up. I don't want to put myself through that kind of heartbreak again. Do you?"

I shook my head. "No, I'd rather not."

"When you told me you liked me last night, I figured you were hallucinating from that fever. But it made me realize that I like you too."

I looked up at him and squeezed his hand. "Isn't that a good thing?"

"It would be if things were different. It's all happening too soon. I need to sort my life out first, be on my own for a while and figure out what I want in life. I think we might've gotten carried away. We both knew this boyfriend-girlfriend thing wasn't real and only temporary and yet I started to believe that it was real, that I had real feelings for you. I like you, Holly, but we need to draw the line here."

I closed my eyes and wiped away the tears making their way down my face. He was right. We had both started to believe in our fake relationship a little too much.

"You're right. We've been fooling ourselves. It was fun while it lasted, though," I said.

His features softened and he bent down. He caressed my cheek with his thumb and kissed me. Careful at first, then more urgent, until I almost lost my mind. But he pulled back before that could happen.

"You were the best fake girlfriend a guy could wish for," he said.

New tears formed in the corners of my eyes, even though I didn't know why. It wasn't like Noah was breaking up with me, as we were never a real couple to begin with. But then why did it hurt so much to hear him say there was no future for us?

"If it means anything, you were the best fake boyfriend as well."

"Should we give each other feedback?" he asked, lightening the mood.

I let my head fall back and laughed. "Gosh, no. I don't want to hear about my annoying traits."

"You don't have that many," he said with a big grin on his face.

"Not that many?"

He looked me in the eye and smiled. "You know I'm only joking. Although..."

"What?"

He averted his gaze. "It's not important."

I put my hand on his cheek and made him face me again. "That's not fair. You need to tell me."

"Fine. Do you realize you always give everyone else the best of you except the people who are right there with you?"

"What are you talking about?"

"Your career. You are always present, physically, but you're glued to that camera of yours. Your followers and fans always get the best of you. I think if you have a boyfriend, he'd like to be the one who gets the best of you."

I swallowed. "Wow. No one has ever said that to me. Do you think that's how everyone feels when they're around me?"

"Don't worry about that right now, Holly. You need to sleep. Dealing with food poisoning is exhausting for your body."

I crawled back into bed.

"Will you stay with me? At least until morning?"

"Of course. We're friends. I'm here for you."

"Do you still have that food lying around somewhere?" I asked.

Noah got up and walked over to my desk. He picked up a plate with two bread rolls and unwrapped the foil before handing them over. "Enjoy."

"Thank you."

I took a big bite and hoped the food would stay inside this time. I offered Noah the second bread roll and we both munched in silence. After finishing my roll, I closed my eyes and immediately drifted off.

When I woke up again, the sun was shining through the curtains and Noah was standing near the door.

"Where are you going?" I asked.

"I'm going for a run on the upper deck. You get some more sleep. I'll see you later, Holly."

He opened the door, closed it with a loud thud and then he was gone before I could tell him goodbye.

CHAPTER THIRTEEN

*I*t was almost two in the afternoon when I finally felt human enough to step outside of my room again. I didn't want to waste my last day at sea inside my cabin. I decided to take it easy and read a book by the pool, but not after I'd at least tried to get a hold of the people who'd hosted the salsa workshop back in Cozumel.

I went to a guest services desk and told the staff member what had happened.

"No worries, let me call them for you," she said.

I let out a relieved sigh. At least one thing was going right today.

The staff member turned away to make the call, but reappeared only moments later. "I'm sorry, but I got an automated message that said the place is closed today."

"Oh, I see. Thanks anyway," I said.

I rode the elevator to the lido deck, bummed out not to be getting my things back. All I could do was wait until we were back on dry land again.

As I settled into one of the beach loungers with a fresh fruit salad, I let my gaze wander. There was a lot I hadn't tried out yet, like the water slides and the zip line. One week on this ship had been way too short to explore the entire vessel. But going on another cruise just to go down a cool water slide? I wasn't up for that either. It wouldn't be the same without Noah anyway.

The sun was doing its best to shine, and about every ten seconds someone got deposited into the pool through the tubes of the water slide, which spanned a couple of decks.

All around the lido deck, I spotted loved-up couples walking hand in hand or sharing a cocktail. I sighed. The promise of finding love on the *Aphrodite* hadn't exactly come true for me, but at least it had for others.

"Mind if I join you?" Georgia's soft voice pulled me out of my thoughts.

"Sure, go ahead," I said.

She put a towel on the lounger next to me and sat down. "How are you, honey? Noah told us you had food poisoning?"

"It's true, sadly. But I'm starting to feel better now. Noah took good care of me."

"I bet he did," she said with a wink.

"You know we're just friends, right?" Even though I'd told her before we were only faking it, Georgia didn't seem to want to believe me.

She laughed as if I'd said something absolutely crazy. "Keep telling yourself that. When I look at you two, I see two people who are nuts about each other. You know, like in those cartoons where the heart eyes pop out?"

"I hate to disappoint you, but we agreed last night that nothing can happen between us."

Georgia raised her eyebrows. "You did?"

"We both only just came out of long relationships. We need time to process everything first, find out who we are."

"What a load of rubbish."

"It's true."

"Find out who you are? What a lame excuse. You can get to know yourself even when you're in a relationship with someone."

Now it was my turn to raise an eyebrow. "It's a case of bad timing and all. We only pretended to be in love. None of it was real."

Georgia patted my arm and shook her head. "So you're telling me you don't have feelings for Noah? That it was all an act?"

"Well, I wouldn't say I have no feelings whatsoever for him. Just that it's not possible for us to be together. We're too different. He lives on an island, and I travel the world. We'd never even see each other. And what if it doesn't work out? It's way smarter for us to end things here."

"You kids make everything far too difficult. Why not take a chance on love? If it doesn't work out, it doesn't. So what if your heart might get broken again? Yes, it stings, but it happens to the best of us. Heck, it took me fifty years to find the love of my life. But once you do, it'll be worth all the heartbreak."

I shrugged. "Maybe if we met during a different time in our lives, I don't know."

"Don't let him get away because you're afraid of getting hurt," Georgia said, looking over my shoulder at something.

I turned around and saw Noah standing there. I waved at him, but immediately lowered my hand when I realized he was greeting someone else. A woman. He laughed at something she said, then walked off toward the pool bar with her.

I didn't know why I was surprised. He was a great catch. And we weren't together, so he owed me nothing. But then why did I feel like someone had just put a dagger through my heart and twisted it with sheer force?

"That look speaks volumes," Georgia said.

"What look?"

"Like you're consumed by jealousy and disappointment. Don't worry though. That woman's no match for you. He might look like he's having fun, but his heart belongs to you. I'm sure of it. Besides, they're talking shop. We met her at breakfast. She's a property lawyer."

"Oh."

Georgia slid her sunglasses over her eyes and got a book out of her bag. "At least tell him how you feel before he goes back home."

Out of the corner of my eye I could see Noah and the woman he was with sipping cocktails. Why did it bother me so much? Noah could talk to whomever he wanted.

I closed my eyes and went over the last twenty-four hours in my head. Noah had taken care of me in the sweetest way possible and I had accused him of not being trustworthy, because he had forgotten my stuff. What had gotten into me? I shouldn't have pushed him away. I should've thanked him for not leaving me in that bathroom in Cozumel.

I got up and told Georgia I was going for a walk. Even though I was still feeling weak after being down with food poisoning, I needed a good sweat to clear my head. I took the elevator to the upper deck and stepped onto the running track.

The rhythm of my feet touching the ground calmed me enough to see things more clearly. I let my mind wander. Maybe Georgia was right after all. It was time I got completely honest with myself.

I dreaded going back home without Noah there to make me laugh or talk to about silly things. I wanted to spend more time with him and get to know him better.

It was true that Kyle's nasty behavior had made me afraid of ever trusting anyone again, but did that mean I should let my fears get in the way of love?

I deserved to be happy. To be with someone who loved me

for who I was. Someone who laughed at my jokes and got on stage for a room full of people to take part in a silly dating show, even though he wanted nothing more than to be left alone. Someone who wasn't grossed out when I vomited all night long after getting food poisoning from a bad burrito. Someone who cared enough about me to cancel his plans and take me to see a doctor. Someone whose kiss made my toes curl. Someone like Noah.

I thought of the first time Noah had kissed me. The memory lit everything inside of me on fire. My feelings for him ran way deeper than I'd dared to admit, there was no question about it.

Gosh, I'd been so stupid not to see all of the signs that were right in front of me. I was in love with Noah. I couldn't let him leave this ship before he knew how I felt about him, even if he didn't feel the same way about me. My heart was already on the line anyway, so I had nothing to lose.

With renewed energy, I ran toward the elevators and pushed the button to the Ultra VIP deck. I had a plan and I wasn't going to let my fears stop me from executing it.

$$\mathbb{C}$$

"Look, I don't know her last name. But I swear she knows who I am. Can't you look her up in your system?"

I nervously tapped my foot on the carpeted floor as I waited for the crew member to give me access to Patricia's suite. I understood they had privacy and security policies to follow, but I presented no danger at all. Surely Benito could see that?

The guy hesitated for a moment, then started typing.

"Okay, I've found her in the system, but I can't let you through. This part of the ship is closed off for other passengers, even VIP ones like yourself."

"I swear I'm harmless, but I understand your concerns. Can't you call her and tell her Holly from *That Backpacking Chick* is waiting for her? If she doesn't want to come over here, I promise you I'll leave."

"Fine," Benito said, probably worried I'd stay put for the rest of the day if he didn't let me have my way. He dialed a number and I prayed Patricia would pick up.

After he passed on my question, there was a silence and then he put down the phone. I expected him to tell me to take a hike, but instead he got up and unlocked the double glass doors in front of us with his key card.

"She'll be waiting for you in the Star Lounge."

In a moment of sheer happiness, I hugged Benito while thanking him profusely and he started laughing. "Well, I'm glad to have been of service, miss. Have a nice day."

"You too," I called and followed the signs to the Star Lounge.

As I entered, I almost tripped over my own feet. The lounge looked out at the lower decks and the floor-to-ceiling windows offered a magnificent view of the open ocean. There was a glass chandelier hanging from the ceiling, right above a collection of velvet sofas and chairs.

Patricia waved me over to a table next to one of the big windows. She was sipping champagne, a fashion magazine spread out in front of her.

"Holly, how can I help you?" she asked as if we were old acquaintances.

I slid down in one of the chairs. "Well, I have a huge favor to ask. It involves Evan Parker."

She folded her hands and leaned back in the chair. "I'm listening."

CHAPTER FOURTEEN

I left my meeting with Patricia with a big smile and a full stomach from the healthy dinner she'd treated me to, but when I stepped into the elevator, nerves rushed through me.

Had I made the right decision or was I crazy for coming up with a plan like that? I shook my head. This had to work and I had no time to doubt myself. In fact, I was running out of time.

I rushed back to my room, slipped into the one fancy dress I'd brought with me and applied some make-up. With my phone still somewhere in Mexico, I had no way of knowing if Noah would be at the amphitheater tonight, so I had asked Benito to call Georgia's room and relay a message to her.

Patricia had also helped me come up with a plan for my vlogging deadline. She'd suggested I make a "best of" video for next week's deadline instead of one about the cruise. It would give me ample time to get the footage Georgia and the others had filmed during their stay and turn it into a cruise compilation video.

The hallway near the amphitheater was packed with people, just like it had been on that first night when I'd dragged Noah on stage with me. It had been an absolutely amazing evening, one I hoped would become a fond memory for us.

I slipped into the room to take a look at the audience. In fifteen minutes, the talent show would start and it would be all or nothing for me. The room was packed with people wanting to enjoy their last night on the cruise with a great show and nerves raced through me. What if I made a fool of myself? Or worse, what if it turned out Noah had told me the truth about not having any romantic feelings for me?

I took a deep breath and tried to get my hands to stop shaking. For a moment, I got scared Patricia wouldn't show, but she arrived as promised and led me backstage.

"I've talked with the show manager and you're good to go. Evan is excited as well. He agreed right away when I asked him. Said helping love find a way is his favorite thing. I didn't even have to bribe him with your offer of coming to stay at your friend's private island."

I let out a sigh. "That's good to hear."

As soon as I'd remembered Evan Parker was going to be a guest performer at the talent show, I had made it my mission to try to get on stage with him. It was a good thing Patricia was a fan of my work or I'd never have even been able to make Evan an offer.

I had told Patricia my entire story, of how Noah and I met and how I needed him to realize that I wanted to give him the best of me. I had even told her Evan could stay at Noah's private island for a week, away from the masses. I had no clue how Noah would react to that, but it was all I could think of. What else did I have to offer someone like Evan that would persuade him to sing a duet with me?

I drew the curtain back with my hand and scanned the room. My heart skipped a beat when I saw Noah and the gang at the back, trying to find an empty seat. I had asked Georgia to make sure Noah would be there. He was crucial for the success of my plan.

As they all took a seat, a sense of gratitude washed over me. How lucky was I to have met such a fun bunch? Robert adjusted his life vest, bringing a smile to my face. No matter how silly he looked, his safety measures were adorable.

Logan traipsed in behind Trina. His white socks were pulled up to his calves, a beige-colored sweater neatly draped around his shoulders. He gave Noah a short nod before sitting down next to him.

George and Georgia were the last to sit down, followed by Mindy. Georgia looked almost as excited and nervous as I was. Gosh, I was going to miss her.

Five minutes later, the emcee walked on stage and introduced the first act.

"You ready for this?"

I spun around and almost bumped into Evan. "As ready as I can be. Thank you so much for doing this for me. I know I'm a stranger to you. I really appreciate it."

He pushed a hand through his hair and smiled, the dimples in his cheeks deepening. "When I met you earlier this week, you told me to check out your channel and I did. So I guess I do know you a bit."

"You checked out my channel?"

He put the strap of his guitar around his neck and plucked at the strings. "I love traveling. But I can't travel without a bodyguard anymore and especially not to known places. So I guess your channel enables me to live vicariously through you."

My heart almost exploded at his kindness. "I can't believe Evan Parker likes my work," I said.

"Give yourself some credit, girl. Of course I like your work. Now, let's sweep that guy off his feet and make him yours, 'kay?"

"Yes." I took one more deep breath before following Evan on stage.

The crowd went crazy, but it didn't seem to shake Evan one bit. With confident strides, he walked toward the microphone and started strumming his guitar. I followed suit and took my place in front of the other mic. My hands were shaking and for a split second I wanted to run, but then my eyes met Noah's surprised look. I stayed right where I was.

"Good evening, everyone," Evan said and the crowd grew silent. "I have a girl with me tonight who has a special message for a certain guy. She'll be singing a slightly adapted version of *Nothing Like This* with me tonight. Let's give it up for Holly."

The cheering and clapping of the audience filled the room, but I could only focus on one thing. Noah.

Evan winked at me and started playing the famous opening riff to *Nothing Like This*. He sang the first verse and when he got to the chorus, I jumped right in.

I have known love before,
but it was nothing like this.
Your love makes me come alive
and I promise,
you'll always get the best of me.

As I sang the adapted lyrics, Noah's face lit up in recognition until his smile reached his eyes. The cheers of the crowd pushed me to take it one step further and I took the microphone out of the stand. I motioned to Noah to join me on stage. He shook his head, but Georgia pushed him out of his seat. He made his way through the rows of people to reach the front of the amphitheater.

One of the crew members helped him on stage and I walked over to him. When Noah stood right in front of me, Evan stopped singing. He kept strumming his guitar though and I looked Noah right in the eye while I sang the chorus again. When I got to the last lyric, he shook his head and took a step closer, picking me up by the waist and spinning me around. The crowd went wild and everyone got up on their feet, whistling and cheering.

"You're crazy, Holly."

I put the mic back in the stand and beamed at Noah. "I know you said we can't be together, that the time isn't right and that you need to find yourself first. But I can't let you go, Noah. I'm in love with you and this is me giving you the best of me. I might be nuts for doing this, but I want you to know that I'm crazy about you."

He grinned and put me down again. "Well, it's a good thing I'm just as crazy about you then."

And while Evan kept singing *Nothing Like This*, Noah's mouth found mine and he kissed me like I had never been kissed before.

EPILOGUE

"*I*s that the last of the boxes?"

"Yup. That's all."

Noah shut the door of the van and joined me on the sidewalk. He put his arms around me and I let my head rest against his chest while looking up at the building in front of us.

"I'm going to miss this place," I said.

"You are?"

I chuckled. "I won't miss the arguing couple next door or the moldy staircase. But we did share some great times here, didn't we?"

Noah bent down and caressed my cheek before planting a soft kiss on my lips. "The best. But I know we'll make even better memories on Stingray Isle."

I smiled at the name Noah had given his private island. He said he wanted the island to remind him of our first kiss together.

For the last six months, Noah and I had rented a tiny apartment together while Noah arranged the property transfer of the island and I was busy setting up the deal with Big Bear Co. Now that everything was settled, there was nothing keeping us in

Miami anymore. We were going to spend the winter months at Stingray Isle, just the two of us. And after that? Who knew. I was open to whatever possibilities came our way, as long as it meant the two of us being together.

"Ready to go?" Noah asked.

"Definitely. Let's get out of here," I said and we walked toward the van.

Noah let go of my hand and got behind the wheel.

"I love you, Holly," he said before turning on the ignition.

"Right back at you."

I held my hand up in front of me to marvel at the sparkling diamond on my finger. I glanced over at Noah and sighed. I was one lucky girl.

As we drove away, *Nothing Like This* blasted through the speakers. This was the beginning of the best adventure of my life.

Read on for a sneak peek at *I Saw Him Standing There* by Holly Kerr, the first book in the Oceanic Dreams series!

SNEAK PEEK - I SAW HIM STANDING THERE

HOLLY KERR

Day One: Miami

I had one leg out the window by the time the banging started at the door.

I knew Eduardo was coming today but I thought I'd have more time. When I first met him, Eduardo used to be known as Fast Eddie. This con, the one he was coming to collect for, was supposed to be the one to bring us to the big leagues.

The problem was, I didn't want to go to the big leagues. And I had no idea how to tell him I hadn't been able to go through with his latest confidence scam. There was nothing for him to collect and a whole lot to clean up after.

I sat on my bedroom window ledge, the cement scratching the backs of my legs, and contemplated my options.

It was only a short swing from the ledge over to the balcony next door, only a short four-story drop if I fell.

The banging inside was getting louder. "Siggy! I know you're in there!"

I winced, tightening my grip on the window frame. Eduardo

does not sound happy. He was expecting me to meet him at the door with smiles and a stack of bearer bonds I was supposed to have acquired.

No smiles. No bonds.

Our carefully laid plan had gone horribly, terribly wrong, all because I had been struck by an attack of conscience.

"Siggy! Open the door!"

With a deep breath, I turned on my belly and hung from the ledge by my fingers. Swinging my legs to get enough momentum, I flew across to the other ledge, landing awkwardly with the heavy backpack and my camera bag slung across my chest.

I could lose the backpack, but the camera went everywhere with me.

The jump down onto the neighbouring garage was relatively easy compared to the first part, as was the next drop. Eduardo stuck his head out my bedroom window as I landed easily on the cracked sidewalk.

"I want my money, Siggy!"

"I don't have it," I called up to him.

"You better be on your way to get it."

With a last glance, I took off down the street, Eduardo's bellow of rage following me.

Andy's car was parked around the corner from my apartment. With a quick glance behind me, I popped the lock with the handy bent coat hanger I shoved in my bag for that very reason. With a silent promise to see the car back to Andy, I climbed in and twined the right wires together under the dash. The car roared to life.

I was out of the neighbourhood before Eduardo could huff his way down the street, leaving Surfside behind me with barely a hint of remorse except a sinking feeling in my stomach.

Beaches and palm trees flew by as I drove. I didn't stop until I passed the Lincoln Mall in South Beach.

Once I passed the mall, I deemed it safe to stop and called Andy. "I took your car," I confessed as soon he answered. "I'll get it back to you. I promise."

I heard noises in the background, Andy rummaging in his closet-sized apartment to find his keys. "I didn't take your keys." Another skill I'd learned from Eduardo. There had been talk of me becoming some kind of Baby Driver, like in the movie, but the arrest of one of Eduardo's friends after an easy liquor store heist had put an end to that.

Andy sighed. "What did he do to you?"

When I arrived in Miami four years ago, I was on my way from transforming myself from the empty-headed party girl who let a man get close enough to take advantage of me and my family, to a badass who wouldn't stand for it. I no longer wanted to be Seraphina Park-Smith; daughter, sister, wife. I said goodbye to my old life and became Siggy Smith, using the nickname my brother had given me as a child.

Eduardo had taught me ways to survive and thrive on my own. Quite a few of those skills skirted the lines of legality while some of them were just morally questionable. I went along with it because I'd been mad and looking for a way to get revenge.

Then the desire for revenge faded and I was left with only two things: the realization I'd become someone I didn't like very much; and Eduardo, who liked who I'd become a little too much.

"I thought last night was to be the big score," Andy said when I didn't answer.

"I couldn't do it." There was a tiny nugget of pride that I hadn't gone through with the plan. "There were kids involved. Eduardo's not going to understand."

"No, I daren't say he will. But I get it. You're not that person, my darling. You don't fit in with us, as much as you try."

"You could have told me sooner!"

"I thought you were happy."

Had I been happy learning the ropes to become a con artist? It had been fun at first, but then it started being serious. I found myself out of options when I snipped the family purse strings.

"I don't know where to go," I admitted.

"You could go back to your family," Andy said in a quiet voice. "You know they'll have forgiven you by now."

"I doubt it." The coolness in my voice covered the longing.

"Think about it. And be careful with my car. Send me a text where you end up and I'll come and fetch it."

"Thank you. I'm sorry."

"For what? Not pulling off the scam? I would have been sorrier if you had. Love you, darling. And I'm proud of you. Whatever happens."

Andy had become my family and had been since he found me shivering at the airport three and a half years ago, all my worldly possessions in my bag, dried tears streaking through my makeup. I had been a perfect mark but instead, he took me in and took care of me.

I was glad I hadn't let him down.

I said goodbye and tucked my phone into the cupholder, wondering what to do now. The backdoor of the car opened.

I glanced around in horror, expecting Eduardo, the cops, my father, anyone but a woman. Prada shades covered most of her face, and she held a glittery phone in her hand. With an exasperated huff, she swung a Louis Vuitton carry-on into the backseat. "A little help would be nice."

I could only stare at her. "I'm not a cab."

"You have an Uber sticker on your window."

Darn it. I forgot Andy sidelined as an Uber driver. "But I'm not—this isn't my car." What was I supposed to do, admit I stole the car? "I'm not on duty right now."

"Just drive me to the cruise terminal and you can call it a day." She plunked her handbag on her lap and my gaze lasered in on it. Kate Spade Maise Satchel in hot pink.

My heart hurt for a moment at the sight of the bag. "I like your bag."

"Of course you do. Put my suitcase in the trunk and then drive."

"I can't put it in the trunk. It's—ah—broken." Or unavailable because I had no key.

She lowered her glasses. "What do you mean, broken?" She glanced around Andy's ten-year-old Toyota with a disdainful expression. "What kind of Uber car is this?"

"I mean, not *un*broken. I can't get into it. So you should get another ride."

"Do you have a body in there or something?"

I lowered my own cheap plastic sunglasses and gave her a look. Her eyes widened and I thought she was really going to jump out of the car. Then I relented. "No body. Just broken. I'll put your suitcase in the back seat."

I didn't know why I agreed. Maybe because I didn't have a plan, and I needed one. I couldn't keep driving aimlessly.

"So where to, once you get to the port?" I pulled away from the curb. Miami Port wasn't too far, enough to give me enough time to make a plan. I could head to the bus terminal and—

"It's me."

I thought she was talking to me until I glanced in the mirror and saw her holding her phone to her ear.

"I have to go; it's all booked. No, I'm not looking forward to it. No, I'm sure it's going to be horrible. Seven days at sea with obnoxious strangers. It's going to be hell."

Hell was this drive with the obnoxious stranger in the backseat.

She paused in her conversation and from the scowl on her face, apparently didn't like the response she was getting.

"It's some sort of love cruise. You board, you fall in love, or you stay in love, or something silly like that. Like being on a boat is some sort of magic spell. *It's not.*"

"Turn down the music."

It took her asking—demanding, rather—twice more before I realized she was talking to me.

"Don't you love this song?" The music was a bit loud but that was how I liked to drive.

"No, I really don't and it's difficult enough to have this conversation without Kelly Clarkson blaring in my eardrums."

Some people were not nice. There are all sorts out there—nasty, rude and basically horrible people live in this world. I didn't know why they were like that, but they are and no matter how nice and considerate you are back to them, it really makes no difference.

This woman was like that. I didn't know who she was talking to on the phone but I wish they'd wise up and hang up on her and let me do my Good Samaritan deed in quiet. With Kelly Clarkson blaring in my eardrums.

But you know what they say about no good deed going unpunished.

I was punished from outside the car as well. Traffic was terrible, definitely not helpful when I was running for my life.

I thought about how Eduardo's face puffed up tomato red when he was angry. And I remembered when Jimmy had his knee problem that happened the same time the deal he was doing with Eduardo fell through.

Yep. It was definitely time to get out of Miami.

My mind was foggy with ominous thoughts as I drove towards the port of Miami, the one-sided conversation in the backseat fading into the background. But the chime of her cell got my attention, as did her excited gasp.

"Oh! Peter!"

She sounded so different that I glanced in the rearview mirror to see a woman transformed. She was smiling and when she pulled off her sunglasses, there were actual tears in her eyes. "I'm so glad you called." She *cooed* into the phone like she was talking to a baby.

Or a man.

"Okay. Okay. Okay, okay...yes...okay... Oh, yes!"

I snickered under my breath. Had she forgotten her words?

"Stop the car!"

"We're not at the terminal."

"I said, stop the car. Right now. Here. He'll pick me up."

"Who?" I couldn't help but ask. After all, if I was acting as an Uber driver, then I was responsible for her, wasn't I?

"Peter." She all but sighed.

"Who's Peter?"

"He's *Peter*. Here, stop here. He'll be here soon."

"Should I wait?" If I hadn't turned around, I would have missed the look she gave me. *Of course, you should wait, you moron.*

Even in love, she was still mean.

"Is he going on this cruise with you?" I asked as I pulled over.

"Of course not and now I don't have to go either." She clapped her hands suddenly. Whoever this Peter was certainly put her in a better mood. "I don't have to go!"

"Do you get your money back? I mean, if I'm taking you to the boat, doesn't that mean you're supposed to be getting on it? You can't just not show up for something like that. They may hold the ship for you."

She stared at me. "They won't do that."

"They might." I had no idea if a cruise ship would hold off

sailing if a passenger didn't show up but it was fun to play with her.

"They might for me," she agreed. "Here." She rummaged in her Kate Spade and pulled out a slim black leather portfolio. Taking out a handful of papers, she thrust them between the seats. "Take my ticket."

"What? No!"

"I'm not going to use them. You might as well."

"They won't really hold the boat for you. I just made that up."

"You'd be surprised how many people wait for me."

"I can't use your tickets. I mean, really, I can't. They won't let me. Besides, they're in *your* name." A glance at the papers showed her name was Petra Van Brereton.

"Take my passport."

"Are you kidding me?"

She threw it into the front seat. "I'll get another one. You look enough like me that no one will notice. It's always a hassle boarding; you can slip right through. And you'd be doing me a favour. My parents are going to be furious when they find out about Peter. This way we can get married and they'll think I'm still on the cruise and won't even look for me."

I glanced at her picture. Other than both of us having brown hair, we really looked nothing alike.

I started to hand the documents back but then stopped. Eduardo would never find me in the middle of the ocean. And I'd be doing her a favour. I knew all about upsetting parents.

"My uncle is the captain. I'll call him and clear everything. Use my passport to get on, and then everything will be fine."

"I don't know..."

"Seriously, take it. I don't need them. It's a love cruise—"

"Like the *Love Boat*? You know, that television show from the seventies?" I asked. Her expression changed to annoyed confusion. "It must be on Netflix by now."

"I have no idea what you're talking about. Take the tickets. Take my bag. Go on the cruise. Have a nice life."

I took the tickets.

What else was I supposed to do? She wasn't going to use them, and it was better than wasting them.

Petra was too busy kissing the tall, handsome man to notice when I pulled away with her suitcase. The tickets for the cruise lay on the passenger seat.

I promised myself I'd return Petra's passport as soon as I got back.

When I pulled up to the terminal, I saw a big, beautiful boat docked at the pier with crowds of people on deck.

The *Oceanic Aphrodite*.

If this was really some sort of love cruise, at least it had a good name.

⚲

Grab I Saw Him Standing There now at Amazon!

⚲

Dear reader, thank you so much for reading this book. I hope you loved it as much as I loved writing it. Feel free to leave a review on Amazon or Goodreads. It doesn't have to be long. A couple of sentences are great too.

I love staying connected with my readers and showing them what goes on behind the scenes. Feel free to follow me on Instagram, Facebook, Bookbub or Goodreads.

If you want to stay updated and claim a free short story, featuring the main character of The Best of You, please subscribe to my newsletter here: http://www. sophieleighrobbins.com You'll also get the chance to apply for my ARC team.

ACKNOWLEDGMENTS

Writing this book was a fantastic experience. I couldn't have done it alone, though!

First and foremost, thank you to the other amazing authors in this series: Holly Kerr, Laura Heffernan, Tracy Krimmer, Kirsty McManus, Holly Tierney-Bedord, Delancey Stewart, and Monique McDonell. It was great working on this project together!

Kirsty McManus. A big thank you for everything you have done and continue to do for me. I'm blessed to have you in my life.

Serena Clarke, thank you for editing this book. It wouldn't be as good as it is without your help. It's always a pleasure working with you.

Evie Antonis, thank you for beta reading and giving me feedback. And for supporting me throughout!

Thank you to my friends and family for their ongoing support.

To Hugo: you guys rock! And to my girlfriends: you are golden! I love you all.

To my other amazing friends who support me in any way: thank you so much!

A special thank you to my grandmother for believing in me, even though you don't understand what eBooks are all about. You're one of my biggest fans and I love it!

And last, but not least, thank you to my husband for enabling me to write, for always supporting me, and for loving me unconditionally.

ALSO BY SOPHIE-LEIGH ROBBINS

THE OCEANIC DREAMS SERIES

Printed in Great Britain
by Amazon